Ghost Buddy

HENRY WINKLER is known worldwide for his role as the Fonz on the series *Happy Days*. He is also an award-winning producer and director of family and children's programming, and the author (with Lin Oliver) of the Hank Zipzer series (Walker Books). Henry is a passionate advocate for child literacy in the UK and in 2011 was awarded an OBE. He lives in Los Angeles, California.

LIN OLIVER is a television producer and writer, who co-authored (with Henry Winkler) the *New York Times* bestselling Hank Zipzer series as well as many of her own titles. Lin lives in Los Angeles, California.

Henry Winkler & Lin Oliver

Ghost Buddy

Zero to Hero

■SCHOLASTIC

To Debra Dorfman, whose favourite word is "yes".
And to Stacey always. —H.W.

For Debra Dorfman, who brought
Ghost Buddy alive. —L.O.

Scholastic Children's Books
An imprint of Scholastic Ltd
Euston House, 24 Eversholt Street
London, NW1 1DB, UK
Registered office: Westfield Road, Southam, Warwickshire, CV47 0RA
SCHOLASTIC and associated logos are trademarks and/or registered
trademarks of Scholastic Inc.

First published in the US by Scholastic Inc., 2012
First published in the UK by Scholastic Ltd., 2012

Zero to Hero © Henry Winkler and Lin Oliver, 2012
Cover art © Tony Ross, 2012

The right of Henry Winkler and Lin Oliver to be identified as
the authors of this work has been asserted by them.

ISBN 978 1 407 13228 0

A CIP catalogue record for this book
is available from the British Library.

Printed and bound by CPI Group (UK) Ltd, Croydon, CR0 4YY

Papers used by Scholastic Children's Books are made
from wood grown in sustainable forests.

3 5 7 9 10 8 6 4

This is a work of fiction. Names, characters, places, incidents and dialogues are
products of the author's imagination or are used fictitiously. Any resemblance
to actual people, living or dead, events of locals is entirely coincidental.

www.scholastic.co.uk/zone

Chapter 1

Billy Broccoli wasn't getting out of the car. He had warned them. In fact, he had spent a month and a half warning them. Forty-five days to be exact. He had said, "You can move to the new house. I support that decision wholeheartedly. Just don't ask me to move with you. I can't and I won't."

"Billy, that's enough," his mother said, tapping her foot impatiently. "You've made your point. Now get out of the car."

"No, thanks, Mum."

"Billy. I understand how you're feeling. It's normal for a child to resist change." His mother, Charlotte Broccoli-Fielding, was a middle-school head teacher and knew all there was to know about eleven- to thirteen-year-olds. Or so she thought. The only hole in her knowledge was her own son.

"First of all, Mum, I am no longer a child," Billy said to her. "I'm eleven going on twelve, which makes me officially a tween. Not only do we have our own television shows, but I have my own mind . . . which, by the way, is insisting that I stay in the car."

Billy rolled up the window to end the conversation.

"Well," Dr Bennett Fielding said, "I guess Bill has certainly let us know where he stands. Let's give him some time, and I'm confident he'll make the right decision and come in the house."

Dr Fielding was Billy's new stepfather, having married Billy's mother only eleven days before. He had a lot to learn about how stubborn Billy could be.

His daughter, Breeze Fielding, Billy's new thirteen-year-old stepsister, knew differently.

She had seen Billy's stubborn streak in action when, at their parents' wedding, he refused to wear the shiny shoes that came with the rented tuxedo and insisted on wearing his baseball boots instead. He said it was a garden wedding anyway, and the boots gave him better traction as he came down the aisle carrying the rings. That was OK with Breeze, though, because at the wedding, she wore motorcycle boots on her feet, blue streaks in her hair and a lot of thrift store velvet in between.

"Come on, folks. Let's go inside," Breeze said. "It's not like he's going to stay in there for ever. As soon as he has to pee, he'll come flying in the front door doing the I-gotta-go dance."

"Point well taken, Breeze," her father answered. "Your thought process is as clean as a well-flossed tooth." Dr Fielding was a dentist, and nothing made him happier than the subject of healthy teeth.

Billy looked out of the window of the car and

studied his new house. It gave him the creeps. Every other house on the block was normal: beige stucco with a lawn at the front, a basketball hoop in the driveway and a brick path leading up to a painted front door. Not this house, though. No, this house had a mini orange grove where the front lawn should be, with actual dead oranges rotting on the ground. Not only did it *not* have a basketball hoop in the driveway, it didn't even have a driveway. Why should it? It was built before cars were invented, when Los Angeles was just a small town by a river. And it looked it, too, with its peeling paint and rusty iron door knocker shaped like the head of a horse. His mother and stepfather said it was an architectural treasure. Billy thought it should be put back in the treasure chest and dropped to the bottom of the river.

It was too late for that, though. The removal van had already arrived, and several burly men were starting to unload the hundreds of boxes that contained the family's entire life. Billy pulled down the armrest and leaned back, watching the neatly labelled parade of cardboard boxes go by. *Pots and Pans, Billy's Baseball Cards, Clean Towels, Towels to Be Washed, Parrot Cage Without Bird, Assorted Hair Products*. Billy knew that box smelled like coconut mango honey, his mum's favourite shampoo scent. He always knew whenever she had just washed her hair, because every bee in the neighbourhood wanted to land on her head.

"Hey, weirdo!"

Billy heard a muffled voice followed by a sharp rat-a-tat-tat on the window. He whipped around and saw a face pressed up against the glass like a suction cup. It was a big, doughy face that spread itself all over the window.

"Your car's back wheel is on our property by fifteen millimetres," the face said. "I just measured it. I'm going to have to report this to the police."

"Pardon me," Billy said. "It's hard to hear what you're saying."

"I said move it or I'm reporting you for trespassing," the face shouted.

Billy rolled down the window just a crack, enough to let sound in. He peered out and saw that the face belonged to a boy about his age, tall and bulky with binoculars around his neck and a retractable tape measure in his hand.

"I will move it," Billy said, "in five years, when I get my licence."

"Oh," the big kid said. "So you're one of those. New, and a wise guy. I'd ask your name, but it's a waste of my time, because you're not going to be in that house long anyway."

"What are you talking about? My parents just bought it."

"The last family stayed a year. The one before that, six months, tops."

"Why? Because they all met you?"

The kid let out a laugh that was something between a snort and a grunt, and sprayed a little snot on the window.

"That was funny, toad face."

"My name's Billy. Billy Broccoli to be exact. I know you're probably going to laugh at that – everybody does – but we just had the car washed, so try to keep yourself from snorting."

"Funny again. That's two for you. I'm Rod Brownstone. And I know everything about this neighbourhood. You don't want to mess with me."

Billy got out of the car, and as he did, he realized that Rod Brownstone was almost twice his size, not only in mouth but in body. Rod's head, which sported a thick cluster of black, lumpy hair, was as big as a small boulder and his body seemed rock hard, too. Billy felt smaller than usual, which wasn't easy because he was short to begin with. Even if his name didn't start with a *B*, he would still have been at the front of the line in school, because he was the shortest boy in class. His mum reassured him that a growth spurt was in his future, but he was starting to seriously doubt that.

Rod picked up his binoculars and focused them directly on Billy.

"What are you looking at?" Billy asked him.

"Just standard police practice when gathering intelligence to keep the neighbourhood safe."

"I'm not exactly a threat, Brownstone."

"I'll be the judge of that," Rod snorted. "Just remember, Broccoli. I've got you in my sights."

Billy backed away from Rod, feeling both intimidated and weirded out. This guy wasn't what you'd call a welcome wagon. In fact, he made Billy even more nervous about his new house than he already was. As he backed up, he bumped into one of the movers carrying a box labelled *Billy's Baseball Gear*. It was upside down and the tape holding the lid closed bulged, as if the contents might fall out any second.

Billy wasn't very good at baseball, but he loved it and always took care of his equipment, in case one day his skills suddenly grew to match his love of the game.

"Excuse me, sir," Billy said. "I'll take that. I don't want my gear to fall."

It was a perfect excuse to get away from Rod Brownstone. The mover shrugged and handed the box to Billy, who took it and hurried up to the front door.

"Well, look who's decided to show up." Breeze stood in the doorway, holding her mobile phone between her ear and her shoulder while spiking her hair in the reflection from the latched glass peephole in the front door.

"I wouldn't be here, except our next-door neighbour was just about to put me under house arrest," Billy said to her.

"I know that kid Rod," Breeze answered. "He's on the football team at school. If I were you, I'd hang out with him and find out what his secret is. Maybe he can un-scrawny-ize you."

"Thanks for the vote of confidence, Breeze. Can you just tell me where my room is?"

"Last one at the end of the hall. We flipped a coin, but a certain somebody was sitting in the car, so you got what you got. Don't worry, it'll grow on you. Or not."

Billy made his way down to the end of the hall. His mother and stepfather were in their room, trying to find enough space in the wardrobe for all their clothes. Like most dentists, Dr Fielding had mostly white short-sleeved shirts, but unlike other dentists, he had an extensive collection of coloured ties, each one featuring a big smiling tooth in the middle. Some even had captions with the tooth saying things like "You drill me!" or "You're so filling" or "Decay Stinks". Dr Fielding thought they were hilarious.

Billy passed by Breeze's room, a large airy space that had its own little patio. When he got to his door, he adjusted his grip on the box, pushed the door open with his rear end, and backed into the room. It was a good thing, too, because had he walked in frontways, he would have taken one look around and passed out right then and there.

The room was lavender and pink. And to make matters worse, there were ponies chasing rainbows on the wallpaper. For furniture, there was a lavender dresser, a pink wicker desk and a bed with a lavender headboard that had the words *Sleep Tight, Sweetie Pie* chiselled into it.

Billy dropped the box, dropped his jaw, and screamed. "It's a nightmare in the middle of the morning!"

"What's the matter, honey?" his mum called as she came running down the hall.

"Mum, this room is having a pink attack."

"I know it's not exactly your colour scheme, sweetie. But don't worry, we have plans."

"Really? To seal it up with brick? Because I'm all in favour of that."

By that time, Dr Fielding had arrived on the scene.

"Bill," he said. "I imagined that you and I would take this on as a do-it-yourself project. You pick the colour, we'll paint it together."

"Can we start, like, now, Bennett, because I can't go in there ever again."

Breeze, hearing the commotion, came down to enjoy the fireworks.

"Hey, you could sleep in the car," she suggested to Billy. "You seem to like it in there. A blow-up mattress, some crisps, and a mini TV? A guy could get used to that."

"This isn't funny, Breeze. I couldn't possibly invite a new friend over to this room."

"And how many new friends do you have exactly? Correct me if I'm wrong, but I thought it was none."

"I have plans to build an army of friends," Billy said.

"I guess that doesn't include your pal next door. You two didn't seem to hit it off."

Breeze's phone rang again and she headed back to her room, laughing and talking with one of her hundreds of friends. Billy envied her. Their new house was in the district she and Bennett had been living in before the wedding, so she didn't have to change schools. She could just continue at Moorepark Middle School with nothing more than a change-of-address form. But for Billy, the move to this house meant everything would be different. He had to leave his old neighbourhood and his old friends and his old school and start all over again – and at Moorepark, where his mother was head teacher. Just the thought of that made his head spin.

Billy decided that some food in his belly might settle him down, so he walked down the hall and headed for the kitchen, hoping his mother had stocked the refrigerator with string cheese and apple juice, his favourite snacks. She had.

The snack made him feel much better and he returned to his room, determined to make himself adjust to the purple mist around him. But his good mood disappeared when he walked in his room. His baseball stuff, including his glove, two aluminium bats, his boots, his shorts, and his three signed game balls, had somehow found their way out of the box and were sitting in a perfectly formed circle on the carpet. This was unacceptable. He tore down the hall, shouting Breeze's name.

"Stop yelling," she said, poking her head out of her room. "What's your problem?"

"Let's get this straight, Breeze. I've only asked you two things since I've known you. One, don't touch my baseball stuff. And two, don't touch my baseball stuff."

"Why would I even want to touch your infested baseball gear? It reeks."

"Don't tell me it wasn't you."

"Billy, I don't know what you're talking about."

"Follow me and I'll show you."

Billy marched Breeze down to his room and pointed to the centre of his carpet.

"There," he said. "I never gave you permission to take my stuff out of the box."

"It's not out of the box, genius."

Billy whipped around and to his utter amazement, all his baseball gear was neatly packed in the cardboard box, and the lid was taped shut.

"Don't bother me again with your stupid jokes," Breeze said. "You're not funny."

Billy didn't answer. He couldn't. All he could do was stare silently at that box. Was he going nuts? He could have sworn that his baseball gear had got out of that box and then put itself back.

But how?

Chapter 2

After Breeze left, Billy stood there staring at the box. He was a logical person and he knew that baseball equipment didn't just unpack and repack itself. As he tried to come up with a rational explanation for this mystery, his mother came into his room, carrying an armload of clothes on hangers.

"Honey, these things need to be hung up in your wardrobe nicely," she said. The stack of clothes was so big that all Billy could make out was the top of her brownish curly hair and the toes of her red cowboy boots. "You start a new school on Monday and you don't want to show up on the first day with wrinkly clothes."

"Just drop them on the rug, Mum. I'll get to it later."

"I want you to start on it right away. Here, I'll show you how."

She flopped the stack of clothes on the pink desk, picked up three or four hangers, and walked towards the wardrobe.

"Mum, this is totally unnecessary. I'm one of the great hanger-uppers."

"Really? What about that pile of clothes in your old room that you referred to as Smelly Mountain? I didn't see much in the way of hanging up going on there."

Mrs Broccoli-Fielding pulled the wardrobe door open and stepped inside. Her nose twitched.

"Billy, you know the rules. You're not supposed to have food in your room."

"Mum, I haven't eaten anywhere but in the kitchen. Honest."

"Then why does your entire wardrobe smell of orange juice?"

Billy walked to the wardrobe and took a whiff. She was right. It smelled like one of those trees in the front garden.

"I guess the girl who had this room before me must have liked to drink orange juice in the wardrobe." He shrugged. "She probably did it to get away from all the purple and pink."

"OK, young man, start hanging," Billy's mum said. "And just to show you that moving day can be fun, we've ordered pizzas for dinner, including your favourite, pineapple bacon."

"Breeze had better not touch that," Billy said, his mouth starting to water.

"Honey, Breeze is vegetarian."

"Since when?"

"Since ten o'clock this morning. She says she feels better already."

Billy's mother left, and with a deep sigh, he started to put his clothes away. The first hanger he grabbed held his baseball jersey from last season. It looked almost new, since mostly he sat on the bench and didn't get to play much.

Billy hooked the hanger on the wooden bar in the wardrobe – but when he turned to get another piece of clothing, he heard a noise that sounded like the hanger scuffling along the bar on its own. Billy glanced into the wardrobe and it seemed to him that his baseball jersey had moved.

No, that couldn't be.

Just to make sure, he turned his back to the wardrobe, then spun around with lightning speed, half expecting to catch his jersey moving by itself. But it just hung there, smelling like orange juice, presenting no danger to anyone.

Billy was relieved, because he was not a guy who loved danger. At the top of his list of least favourite things were scary movies, bumpy aeroplane rides, bungee jumping, roller coasters, creepy or sad clowns and anything that popped up at him. As a matter of fact, when he was five and a half, he'd smashed his jack-in-the-box to bits with his slipper.

He spent the rest of the afternoon putting his clothes away and organizing his room. By the time he finished, ate some pizza, and crawled into bed that night, he was exhausted. But even though he was bone tired, he just couldn't drift off. He missed his old room in his old house. And he worried about starting a new school on Monday and having to make all new friends.

Billy rolled to his side and stared at the wardrobe door, focusing on the brass doorknob. He had read once that if you stared at something for a really long time and didn't even let yourself blink, it calmed you down enough so that you eventually fell asleep without knowing it. He must have stared at that doorknob for seven minutes, but nothing happened. It just hung there on the edge of the door, being all knobby. He was about to give up when suddenly he saw something that made his stomach flip and his blood run cold.

The knob was turning all by itself! Billy closed

his eyes, counted to three, then opened them and focused back on the knob. The knob turned again, as if someone inside the wardrobe was trying to get out.

He tried to call out, "Who's there?" but his vocal cords snapped shut. Nothing came out but a sorry-sounding rasp.

The knob continued to turn. Billy thought he heard the click of the wardrobe door opening.

The next thing Billy heard was the scraping of wood against wood, followed by a long, low creak. Then, with a sudden jerk, the door flew open. Billy pulled the covers over his head, hoping that whoever was in the wardrobe wouldn't see him. Even hidden under the covers, his whole body shook uncontrollably. There was nothing he could do to stop every muscle from twitching.

After a minute, Billy's curiosity got the better of his fear and he peeked out from underneath the covers, exposing only a tiny bit of his left eye. That little piece of eye was enough for him to see the scariest sight he'd ever beheld. The arm of his red and white baseball jersey was reaching out of the wardrobe door, *but there was no hand at the end of the sleeve.*

Billy finally found his voice and shrieked like a five-year-old.

From inside the wardrobe, he heard an urgent teenage voice say, "Shhhh... Do you want to wake the whole house?"

"Yes, I do," Billy rasped. "I absolutely do."

"Trust me, that is something you don't want to do," said the voice.

"I'm going to scream. I can feel it coming up from my toes."

"Calm down, Georgie Boy. You sound like my cousin Annabel when she got bitten by the horse that was pulling the ice wagon."

Billy's head was swimming. Was this a dream or was he actually having a conversation with a sleeve?

"First of all," he ventured, "I don't understand anything you're saying about your cousin what's-her-name and that horse. And second of all, my name is Billy. And third of all, *where* is your hand?"

Suddenly, without warning, Billy's entire baseball jersey flew out of the wardrobe and floated across the room, the red and white sleeves fluttering in the darkness. The jersey came to a stop in front of the mirror on the back of his door. Billy became aware of a strange whirring next to his bed. He whipped around and saw that the numbers on his digital alarm clock were going haywire, spinning like crazy, racing forwards and backwards like some unknown force was controlling them.

Impulsively, Billy grabbed the clock and threw it at the jersey, which was still twisting itself this way and that, looking at its reflection in the mirror. Unfortunately, Billy had forgotten to unplug the clock before he flung it, and it boomeranged back at him, heading right for his face. He ducked just in time to see it land on the floor next to his bed.

"Hey, you'd better pull up on your hand brake, Georgie Boy," the teenage voice said. "Violence is never the answer."

All Billy could think about was that this voice, so confident and so invisible, was coming from an empty, floating shirt.

"Who are you?" he screamed. "Where are you? What are you? *Why are you?*"

The shirt didn't answer. It spun around and headed towards Billy, who had pushed his body flat against the headboard, hoping it would open up and let him escape.

"Do you think these sleeves are too long on me?" the shirt said. "I can't have them interfering when I'm pitching the ball."

"Too long for what?" Billy asked. "You don't have any arms. Or any body, for that matter."

"That's where you're wrong, Georgie Boy."

"Billy."

"Fine, Billy Boy. I have a body. Or at least, I had one before I died. And it was a magnificent sight to behold, if I say so myself. Which I have no trouble doing."

"Are you telling me you're a ghost?" Billy asked. His voice quivered even though he was trying to be composed.

"Ding, ding, ding, ding. Correct answer. You win the prize, a stuffed cow with a full udder."

"Can I just say, in this situation, I'd rather be wrong. Not that I couldn't use a stuffed cow with a full udder."

The jersey let out a laugh that echoed around the room, bouncing from one wall to the other.

"You're funny, Georgie Boy."

"It's Billy. How many times do I have to tell you?"

"I know, I know. It's just that you remind me of a very good buddy I had back in grade school. Georgie Cooperstone. He was a fun kid. We used to sneak out and drive his dad's Model T around the orange groves until we crashed it. Back then, you could drive when you were fourteen. He became a broom salesman and I became a ghost."

"Let me get this straight," Billy said to the shirt. "You're dead? And you've been hovering in my wardrobe for, like, a hundred years?"

"Actually, ninety-nine years. That was when the crash happened. Before that, I lived here."

"In my room?"

"Correction, Billy Boy. Did you notice I got your name right this time? You're living in *my* room."

Billy could not even begin to process what he had heard. He had seen movies about ghosts. Watched cartoons about ghosts. Read comic books about ghosts. But never, in all of his wildest imagination, did he ever think he'd be having a conversation with one.

"I can't believe I'm talking to a ghost," he said.

"That's what most people call me, although I prefer *phantom. Ghoul* works in late October, gives it kind of a Halloween-y flair. What really chaps my britches is when people call me a banshee. I mean, that's just rude."

"If you'll excuse me," Billy said to the shirt, trying to be as polite as possible so the ghost wouldn't attack him, "this is a lot more than I can handle. So hang yourself back in the wardrobe while I take this opportunity to run shrieking out of here."

Rising to his feet, Billy bolted for the door. He was stopped by a chilly pressure pulling on his upper arm.

"Let me make this a little easier for you," the shirt said.

Then it started to whistle "I've Been Working on the Railroad".

"Can't you hear the whistling blowing?
Rise up so early in the morn. . ."

Suddenly, Billy smelled orange juice again, even stronger than when his mother had first detected the aroma in the wardrobe. It was the most tangy, wonderful orange smell you could ever imagine. Then the jersey fluttered and seemed to fill with a human shape. Was that an arm Billy saw, coming out of the sleeve?

The whistling grew louder, the orange smell more powerful. And then . . . out of nowhere . . . he appeared!

Chapter 3

The ghost was a boy about fourteen years old, wearing blousy brown trousers that stopped at the knee. As he pulled off the jersey, Billy could see that his trousers were held up by faded red suspenders, and on his head was a tartan wool newsboy cap with a button on top and a brim that he wore jauntily off to the side. His socks were covered with a pattern of alternating beige and white diamond shapes. On his feet, he wore lace-up work boots of dark brown leather that came up to the middle of his shin. They were laced up only halfway, which instead of looking sloppy gave him a casual, self-assured look.

"I ... I can see you!" Billy whispered in amazement.

"Consider yourself lucky. This is a rare occurrence. Very few people have had the opportunity."

Billy tried to answer, but once again, no words came out. He was looking at a ghost, a real live ghost. Or more accurately, a real dead ghost.

"Because you seem like a nice kid – short but nice – I'm going to introduce myself," the ghost said. "You are in the presence of Hoover Porterhouse the Third. How exciting is that?"

"I'm Billy Everett Broccoli the First. Nice to meet you."

Billy and Hoover went to shake hands, but although Billy's hand was pumping up and down, he could feel only cold air surrounding his fingers.

"This is so weird," he said. "I'm shaking your hand, but I can't feel anything. Just cold air."

"That's the way we ghosts roll. Let me tell you, Billy Boy, it can be pretty frustrating when you dance with a pretty girl and she has no idea you're there. All she does is put on a jumper."

"Wait a minute," Billy asked. "You dance?"

"Not so much any more. But before I died, I could turkey trot with such flair that girls thought there was an actual bird in the room."

With that, Hoover Porterhouse III put his hands under his armpits, folded his arms like turkey wings, and started high-stepping around the room. He didn't stop at Billy's desk or his bed, but danced right through the middle of them.

Before Billy could absorb what he was witnessing, he was tossed up in the air by a massive tremble that felt like an earthquake knocking the house right off its foundation. The tremble was accompanied by what sounded like a freight train charging out of the centre of the earth. If seeing a ghost hadn't been frightening enough, Billy was now officially out of his mind with fear.

From down the hall, he heard Breeze scream, "What is happening here, people? Inform me!" Further down the hall, he heard his parents' footsteps and then their voices calling, "Billy! Breeze! Outside! Immediately!"

"Earthquake!" Billy yelled.

"Trust me. It's not an earthquake," Hoover Porterhouse said to him.

"Oh yeah? What would you call it?"

"Report card day."

Hoover pointed to the wall next to Billy's bed. There, lit up in glowing blue type that seemed to pulsate with the shaking of the house, Billy saw a series of five letters ... C, C, A, F, F. What could those letters mean? And how did they get on the wall of his room?

"This is not fair!" Hoover complained, shaking his fist at the wall. "What do you guys want from me? Well, forget it. I give up. Go ahead and give me two F's. See if I care."

With that, there was another rumble from underground and a huge jolt shook the entire house. It felt like the roof was about to cave in.

"I'm out of here!" Billy shouted to the ghost, who was pacing back and forth and letting out a stream of words that any regular kid would have got ten years' detention for saying. Billy flung the door open and bolted out into the hall. His feet barely touched the floor as he barrelled past Breeze's room and met up with his parents, who were waiting to escort them both out to the front garden.

"This feels like a seven point five on the Richter earthquake scale," Bennett said.

"Whatever the number is, it's totally scary!" Billy answered.

"Children, form a single line and proceed calmly," his mother instructed. "And hold hands."

Years of being a middle school head teacher had prepared Mrs Broccoli-Fielding for any emergency. As the family proceeded in an orderly fashion to the front garden, Billy realized that the house was no longer shaking. The earthquake had hit with a sudden force and disappeared just as suddenly. None of the neighbours were out on the street, and no one but the Broccoli-Fieldings seemed to have experienced this terrifying event.

"Am I the only one noticing that we are alone out here in the middle of the night, in our pyjamas, holding hands?" Breeze asked. Then, turning to Billy, she let go of his hand and said, "I mean this in the nicest way, but your palms are majorly sweaty."

"My hands do that when they're scared," Billy explained. "So do my armpits."

"Nauseous," Breeze said. "If we're going to live in the same house, you've got to filter all armpit talk."

Dr Fielding was poking around the front garden, trying to discover what could have caused the house to shake so violently.

"I don't smell any gas," he yelled over his shoulder.

"Tell the gentleman in the boxer shorts that he can give his nose a rest," a ghostly voice whispered. Billy wheeled around to see Hoover Porterhouse sitting on a branch in one of the orange trees.

"What are you doing here, Hoover?" Billy whispered.

"I followed you out of the house. Hey, that scared me, too. Usually my report card doesn't arrive in such an earthshaking way. The Higher-Ups must have felt they needed to get my attention. I'm assuming they were not overly enthusiastic about my grades."

"Higher-Ups?" Billy whispered. "What are you talking about?"

"You might call them teachers," Hoover explained. "They've been grading my progress for the last ninety-nine years. Apparently, I'm not passing with flying colours. Two C's, two F's, and an A in Personal Grooming, which stands to reason."

Hoover floated down off the orange tree

branch and struck a pose, adjusting his newsboy cap to the side, puffing out his chest, and snapping his red suspenders with his thumbs. "I might be a phantom, but I always look snazzy. It's on my business card. I'm the Ghost with the Most."

Billy was totally perplexed.

"Why do you look so confused?" Hoover said. "Don't you get a report card? I got a C in Haunting Skills, which is unfair. I'm an excellent haunter. I got a C in Invisibility. I'm working on it, but it's not as easy as it looks. It's the F's that really fry my boots, though. One is in Helping Others and the other is in Responsibility. It's too much fun turning people's lives upside down. You can't take that away from a guy."

"OK, it's official," Billy said as Hoover explained the ghostly grading system. "I truly don't understand anything you're saying. My brain is on overload."

"Honey, who are you talking to?" Billy's mum

asked. "You've been muttering to yourself for the last thirty seconds."

"Listen, Mum. This is going to sound weird, but I'm just going to say it flat out. I saw a ghost and he didn't do well on his report card."

"You know what?" Breeze said. "This whole blended family thing isn't working out for me. I can't live in the same house with someone who thinks he's talking to academically challenged ghosts."

Breeze turned and walked back towards the house. Hoover caught up to her and flicked his hand lightly against her hair, which made it seem as if a gust of wind had lifted only one side of her hair.

"Oh, and another thing, Billy," she said, frowning at him. "No one touches my hair."

"I didn't do it. I'm standing over here and you're way over there. What am I, Elastic Man?"

"Then who did it? Your imaginary ghost?"

"Yes, he did."

"Bill," said Dr Fielding, clearing his throat

uncomfortably. "When I was a boy, I had a great imagination, too. In fact, I had an imaginary friend named Tommy Tooth. He was a big beaver with a huge flat tail and two huge pearly whites protruding from his upper gums. I used to fantasize that, one day, I'd fix his overbite, and he'd teach me how to chop wood with my mouth. Sure it was fun, but one day, I realized it was time to give up my imaginary friend and let him paddle his way back into my imagination."

Billy just stared at his new stepfather, speechless. All he could do was nod like a bobble-head doll.

"Thank you for sharing that, Bennett," Mrs Broccoli–Fielding said, taking her husband's hand sweetly. "I'm sure Billy really appreciates your support. But I think what we all need now is a good night's sleep. In the morning, Billy will be able to see that this ghost of his was just a reaction to the stress of moving, combined with tonight's unfortunate furnace rumble."

The family headed through the orange trees

up to the front door. Billy lagged behind. He looked around the front garden for Hoover Porterhouse III, but the only trace of him was the distinctive orange aroma that seemed to accompany him wherever he went.

And even that was getting fainter and fainter.

Chapter 4

That night, Billy tried to go back to sleep, but it wasn't easy. He kept expecting Hoover Porterhouse to float through the window or under the door. But Hoover did not appear. Morning came and sunlight streamed in through Billy's pink ruffled curtains, but there were still no signs of Hoover. When Billy walked into the kitchen for Sunday breakfast, there was no Sunday breakfast, either. His mother was sitting at the table, making a list.

"Hi, honey," she said. "Feeling better this morning?"

"If we can make waffles with peanut butter and maple syrup for breakfast, I'll feel better."

"Of course we can. We just need to go to the

supermarket and get all the ingredients. I'll stock up on a few other things while we're there."

As Billy and his mum climbed into their van, Billy noticed Rod Brownstone hiding behind the hedges, peering out at them through his industrial-size binoculars.

"That's one strange guy," he said to his mum. "He's always spying on us."

"Maybe he's scientific and likes to see things up close. You used to spend all day staring at your ant colony, watching them carry their leaves and twigs through their tunnels."

"Mum, I didn't use binoculars. And besides, we're not ants."

Mrs Broccoli-Fielding started the van, and over the sound of the engine, Billy heard a knock on the passenger-side window. He rolled it down to see a girl of about seven or eight, with pigtails and bright rosy cheeks. She had the same stocky body as Rod, only shorter, so Billy's guess was that she was his sister.

"Hi. I'm Amber Brownstone," she said in a surprisingly raspy voice. "I live next door, and my dad says the sprinklers in the front of your house are broken. My dolls and I are having a fashion show at four o'clock and we're serving hot chocolate with little marshmallows on top, but it's not burning hot, so the marshmallows won't melt."

"Nothing beats a non-melted marshmallow," Billy said, "except maybe a frozen banana."

"I like those, too," Amber giggled. "Covered with chocolate. Do you want to be a judge at our fashion show?"

"Mum," Billy said, shooting his mum a step-on-it look. "We have to get to the supermarket. Like now."

"We'll see you later, Amber," Billy's mum said, putting the van in gear. "And we'd love to come to your dolls' fashion show."

"Speak for yourself," Billy muttered as they pulled away from the kerb.

The supermarket was quiet that early on a

Sunday morning. Billy grabbed a trolley and followed his mum up and down the aisles while she filled it with useful things like canned soup, flour, sugar, bread, maple syrup and butter. She didn't object when he tossed in some of his favourite foods: chunky peanut butter, strawberry jam, frozen waffles, packaged miso soup, tuna fish and cans of little green peas. As they were rounding the corner of Aisle 9 and heading into the paper-goods section, Billy heard the loudspeaker microphone clicking on.

"Good morning, shoppers," a voice said. "I want to introduce you to someone brand-new to the neighbourhood. Billy Broccoli is in the house."

Billy stopped dead in his tracks. He knew that voice. It belonged to a certain ghost he had met the night before. He glanced over at the checkout counter and saw that the microphone for the public address system had left its metal clip holder and was bobbing up and down in mid-air.

"That's him, Mum."

"That's who, honey? You didn't tell me you had already made a friend in the neighbourhood. Oh, look, there's a bakery here right in the supermarket. I'll get some sticky buns while you say hi to your new friend."

And with that, she was off. Billy looked around, but he saw no sign of Hoover. Suddenly, a flurry of plastic picnic plates came flying down the aisle like a bunch of Frisbees heading right towards him. He tried to catch them, but they were coming fast and he could only manage to grab a few out of the air.

"You need to work on your hand-eye coordination, Billy Boy."

Suddenly, Hoover Porterhouse appeared out of thin air. He stood in front of Billy, holding the torn package of plastic plates.

"You wait right here," Billy said to him. "Do not drift. Do not move. Do not fly. I'm going to get my mum so she'll see you and know you're real."

44

"Can't happen, Billy Boy. She won't see me. I'm invisible."

"No, you're not. How could you be? I'm looking at you right now."

"You can see me because I'm your ghost. To everyone else, I'm invisible."

"You're not my ghost! I never asked for a ghost. I asked for an iPod, I asked for my own mobile phone, I asked for a red BMX bike with black trim. But never, on any list, at any time, anywhere, did I ever ask for a ghost."

"Lucky you. I show and you didn't even have to ask. You hit the jackpot, ducky."

Hoover drifted over to the shopping trolley and floated right through the metal slats to perch on the kiddy seat.

"I used to love this stuff," he said, picking up the jar of peanut butter. "Yes, sir, peanut butter was one of the great things about being alive. Everyone in town knew that the Hoove was a peanut-butter hog."

"You call yourself the Hoove? Seriously?"

"No, not seriously. I don't do anything seriously. Bring the cart and follow me. I'll let you feast your eyes on some Hoove-style fun."

Hoover whooshed down the paper-goods aisle, turned the corner, and stopped in front of the seventy-two choices of breakfast cereals. He picked out three family-size boxes and held them in his hands.

"I need your undivided attention," he said to Billy. "First, I will disappear. Second, I will juggle these three boxes."

Hoover began to whistle "I've Been Working on the Railroad", and in the blink of an eye, he disappeared. Suddenly, the three cereal boxes rose into the air and started circling one another, slowly at first, then faster and faster until Billy could barely tell one box from the other.

"Now watch this," the Hoove called out. "I'm going high."

Still circling one another, the boxes rose higher and higher into the air, until they were so close to the ceiling, they actually bounced off the fluorescent light fixtures. Without a doubt, it was an impressive trick.

"Could you stop doing that?" Billy called out. "You're going to get me thrown out of the supermarket."

The three boxes fell from the air, landing in the trolley, one right after the other. Billy looked around for the Hoove.

"Are you still here?" he asked.

"Of course I'm still here," Billy's mother said, returning from the bakery with a bag of sticky buns. Then, glancing in the trolley, she added, "That's quite a lot of cereal for just the four of us."

Billy knew his mother didn't want to hear about his cereal-juggling ghost buddy, so he thought fast.

"I heard on TV that if you go shopping when you're hungry, you buy twenty-two per cent more food," he said. "I guess I should have eaten breakfast first."

After that, Hoover kept himself scarce. He wasn't in the fruit section. Or at the checkout counter. Or in the car park. Billy helped his mum load the shopping into the van and they pulled out of the car park and drove down Ventura Boulevard. When they stopped at a red light near their house, Billy noticed a familiar face outside his window. The strange thing was, it was upside down and sliding down the glass. And if that wasn't enough, it was smiling.

"Hey, ducky," the Hoove said through the glass.

"Mum!" Billy yelled out urgently. "Look out my window and honestly tell me you don't see a face there."

Mrs Broccoli-Fielding slipped her glasses down from the top of her head and looked out of the passenger-side window.

"Listen to me, Billy. What I honestly see is a side-view mirror, some palm trees, a silver parked car and a teenage girl walking along the pavement whose skirt is definitely too short.

What is her mother thinking? Now if you'll excuse me, I have to keep my eyes on the road."

The light changed to green and Mrs Broccoli-Fielding continued down Ventura Boulevard. Hoover had now righted himself to a sitting position and was travelling at the same speed as the vehicle, while holding his cap so it wouldn't blow off in the wind.

"This was a fun little joyride," he called out. "But I've got things to do, places to go, people to see." And with that, he somersaulted back up in the air and disappeared from Billy's view.

One of the Hoove's favourite Sunday excursions was to float into Mrs Moreno's house and rearrange her furniture while she was out for her 1.3-mile jog. She was a slow runner, and that gave him plenty of time to work on at least the living room. But as he headed to her house, he realized that he wasn't in the mood for a prank. He had worn himself out trying to entertain the new kid. In all his ninety-nine years of being a ghost, he had haunted fourteen kids, but he'd never seen one so tightly wound. He was going to have to teach this Billy Broccoli kid a thing or two about having fun if they were going to be roommates.

One thing he knew for sure. If that boy was expecting to start a new school, make friends, and fit in, he was going to have to get something going in the fun department. No one wanted to be around a Goody Two-Shoes like his sister Mary-Margaret had been, who never went anywhere or did anything. And going places was high on Hoover's To Do list. But the Higher-Ups said that until he passed all the subjects on his report card, he couldn't leave the boundaries of his family's original ranchero. The problem was, he kept failing miserably at Responsibility and Helping Others. He was starting to feel the pressure now, because if he didn't pass all his subjects within one hundred years, he'd be permanently grounded. Then he'd be stuck on his family's property for eternity.

But rather than worry about his grades, the

Hoove decided that he was in the mood for a movie. Lucky for him, the Cineplex was within the boundaries that made up the ranchero. Actually, only half of the cinema was, which meant he could only see films that played on screens 1, 3 and 7. The others were off-limits, a rotten break for him because he had never seen any of the Batmans. They always played on Screen 5.

On the way to the cinema, he was distracted by hoots, whistles and screams coming from across the street. Two Little League teams were playing a baseball game in Live Oak Park. If only he could go there, throw a few pitches, and take a few swings, he'd have been the happiest ghost on Ventura Boulevard. But the park was beyond the boundary lines. He'd been warned by the Higher-Ups that if he stepped over the line, he would instantly disappear. Dematerialize. Cease to be.

Hoover watched the kids play for a while but soon became frustrated. When he was alive, he'd been a pitcher for the San Fernando Junior Cougars, way back when baseball was new. Now he could feel his hands itching to throw a fastball. He knew if he stayed there another second, he would zip over the line into the no-man's-land of the park. Then he'd never have a chance to earn his ghostly freedom.

The Hoove put himself into hyperglide and zoomed in the opposite direction. His usual form of transportation was float mode. When he needed to make good time, he went into the Swoosh. But when speed was of the essence, he kicked into hyperglide. He didn't use it all that often because it messed up his hair, but his need to get away from the park was intense, so hyperglide it was.

Since nothing good was playing at the cinema, he decided to return to Billy's house. The Broccoli-Fieldings had just finished eating Sunday brunch at the picnic table in the back garden. The Hoove floated around the table, noticing remnants of pancakes, cheese omelettes, Swedish meatballs in a mushroom cream sauce, and sticky buns scattered on each plate.

"Do you guys ever wonder why a meatball that looks like a meatball is called Swedish?" Billy was asking the other members of the family. "I mean, did some Swedish guy discover the meatball while cross-country skiing?"

Billy picked up a leftover meatball on his plate, held it to his ear, and listened.

"Nope," he said. "I don't hear a Swedish accent."

Billy thought his joke was hysterical, but the Hoove just shook his head. *Any guy who loves meatball humour is going to have a rough go of it at a new school,* he thought.

"Since we're on the topic of meatballs," Breeze was saying, "can I make one tiny suggestion? Let's not have them again. Has anyone here noticed that when they cool off and the sauce congeals, it looks a lot like cow dung?"

"I think they're delicious," Dr Fielding said,

reaching out to his wife and putting his hand warmly over hers.

When Billy excused himself and headed for his room to prepare for the first day of school, the Hoove floated over to his tree. It was an old, twenty-metre-tall live oak tree that stood at the very end of the Broccoli-Fieldings' back garden. The Hoove's father, Hoover Porterhouse II, had planted it when his son was born, and the whole Porterhouse family had referred to it as the Birthday Tree. As the ranch was sold off and houses sprung up where there once had been orange groves, the tree had miraculously escaped the bulldozer. It had always been Hoover's favourite climbing tree, and over the last ninety-nine years, it had become his favourite sitting tree.

He drifted up to the top branch, looking forward to a lazy afternoon spent watching the squirrels scurry around in search of acorns. Suddenly, a strong wind arose and carried him over to the trunk, where he saw a knife chiselling a message into the bark. It said, *Progress Report*.

"Progress report! Already?" The Hoove groaned. "I just got my report card yesterday. Can't you guys give it a rest?"

"Time is running out," he thought he heard the wind say. Then an unseen hand grabbed him by the scruff of the neck and held him.

"OK, OK," he said. "I'll read it. You don't have to get physical."

The knife continued carving until the words *Helping Others* appeared on the tree trunk. The next word the knife wrote was *Fail*.

"Aw, come on," the Hoove argued. "I deserve at least a D. Today I helped a senior citizen find his false teeth. They fell out when he was crossing the street. That's got to count for something."

There was no answer. Instead, the word *Fail* lit up, blinked twice, then disappeared in a blaze of fire, leaving the trunk as if nothing had happened.

"Now I'm never going to see them," Hoover pouted.

The *them* he was referring to were the baseball fields of America. Hoover Porterhouse's dream had always been to see a game at every Major League baseball stadium. It was the one thing he longed for more than anything.

"What am I supposed to do now?" he wondered aloud. "Will you guys please give me a sign?"

At that very moment, Billy Broccoli walked out of the back door of his house, carrying a pair of jeans and a tennis racquet. He threw the jeans over the washing line and started to beat them with the racquet. Dust flew everywhere and scraps of paper and gum wrappers dropped out of the pockets. Billy started to cough and he hacked so hard, it sounded as if he had a fur ball stuck in his throat. His eyes watered, his nose ran and the racquet flew out of his hand as he dropped to the ground, attempting to catch his breath.

The Hoove tried to look away, but the wind kept turning his head so that all he could see was Billy.

"No!" he called out. "I refuse! Please tell me this isn't my sign!"

But it was his sign, and he knew it. The Higher-Ups were speaking to him, telling him that Billy Broccoli was his project. If he ever wanted to see those baseball fields, he was going to have to be responsible and help Billy become the person he wanted to be. Hoover gave a mighty sigh, letting out so much cold air that some of the leaves on the branch actually froze.

He had better start now. There was no time to waste.

Billy Broccoli was no easy assignment.

Chapter 5

By the time the Hoove returned to the house, Billy was back in his room, preparing for his first day of school. The Hoove wafted in through the window and perched himself on top of the bookshelf, the one that was painted in rainbow colours to match the rainbow ponies on Billy's wallpaper. He sat there silently, shaking his head as he watched Billy trying on the clothes he wanted to wear for the first day of school.

First, Billy slipped on a red T-shirt, tucked it into his jeans, and pulled his jeans up high on his waist, the way he liked to wear them. He tightened his belt and put it on the fourth notch, just to make sure that nothing was going to slip. He looked at himself in the mirror, assumed what he thought was an ultracool pose, and nodded with satisfaction.

"Don't even think about it," the Hoove said, startling Billy so much that he might have actually jumped out of his jeans if they hadn't been pulled up almost to his chin.

"I don't see anything wrong with the way I look," Billy said, more than a little insulted.

It was time for the Hoove to get to work. He shot off his perch and, in an instant, stood between Billy and the mirror.

"Let me ask you a direct question, Billy Boy. What do you see when you're staring in that mirror?"

"I see me. Looking pretty good."

"Well, that makes one of us."

"Why? What do you see?"

"First off, I see a guy whose trousers are so high that they might as well be a chin bib, and whose belt is so tight that his voice is going to become soprano any second."

"Are we looking in the same mirror?" Billy

asked. He couldn't believe he was being so thoroughly criticized.

"No, I'm looking directly at you," the Hoove said. "You're anything but a babe magnet. Just look at your T-shirt, for example."

Billy looked at himself in the mirror. The tee, which he had ordered online from his favourite joke T-shirt company, read *VARSITY FARTING TEAM!* The exclamation mark was a little puff of smoke. Billy thought fart T-shirts were hilarious. So hilarious that he owned at least four or five of them.

"This shirt is going to crack everyone up," Billy said. "I'm going to have ten friends before I even get to registration."

"OK," the Hoove said. "Picture this. You walk through the school's front doors for the very first time wearing that shirt. A group of the cutest sixth-grade girls in the twelve western states is standing before you. What do you think happens next?"

"They read my shirt and immediately want to know who the funny new guy is."

"Correction. They read your shirt and run away from you so fast you won't even be able to see their ponytails bobbing up and down in the distance."

"Really? You think so?"

"I know so. I appreciate a good intestinal joke myself, but I am certain that of all the things girls think are funny, expelling gas is not in the top five hundred. So do me a favour. Loosen the belt. Lower the trousers. And show me a shirt with no writing on it."

"What do you know, anyway?" Billy said as he loosened his belt. "You're more than one hundred years old. What was cool back then isn't what's cool now."

"What little you know, Billy Broccoli. Cool is cool. Cool is for ever. I know this because . . . did I mention this? . . . I invented it. My middle name is Cool."

The Hoove floated over to the wardrobe and picked out a dark green T-shirt and a brown hoodie. Billy tried them on together.

"There it is!" the Hoove said, nodded

approvingly. "We're at least on the runway to normal. People might actually want to have a con-ver-sation with you now. And by the way, make sure you don't have any carrots or spinach in your teeth. The Hoove's Rule Number Thirty-three is 'Never approach a social gathering with a vegetable garden stuck in your teeth.'"

"You have a rule for that?" Billy asked.

"I've got rules coming out of my ears, and you're going to benefit from every one of them. Let's start from the beginning. Rule Number One: 'If a dog starts to sniff behind your knees in the presence of a young lady . . . especially a redhead—'"

"Listen, Hoove, I don't care about sniffing dogs and tooth vegetables. I have to organize my notebook for tomorrow."

"Excuse me, I think I'm falling asleep." The Hoove faked a yawn.

Billy sat down at his desk while the Hoove looked around for something more interesting to do. He picked up a Ping-Pong bat and a fluorescent orange Ping-Pong ball on Billy's shelf and started to hit the ball against the wall.

Ping. Pong. Ping. Pong. Ping. Pong.

As the Hoove continued to hit the ball against the wall, Billy noticed that he had great reflexes and never missed a shot. He kept hitting the ball in a perfect rhythm for what seemed like for ever.

"That sound is driving me bananas," Billy said after a while. "Can you give it a rest?"

"Sorry, Billy Boy, I'm in the zone."

"Fine, I'll just leave. After all, it's only *my* room."

"Correction. *Our* room."

"I'm going to the kitchen to make a tuna sandwich for my lunch tomorrow. Try to wrap up your game by the time I get back."

"I can't let you do that."

"What now? Tuna sandwiches aren't cool?"

"No matter how you cut it, tuna fish in a brown bag is going to smell. Your breath is going to reek like a three-day-old sardine. And let me point out that fresh sardines don't smell so great to begin with."

"So then what do you suggest I eat?"

"Listen up to the Hoove's Rule Number One Hundred and Thirteen. You might want to write this down. Acceptable sandwiches include: (1) peanut butter and jelly, but you have to chew slowly. You don't want your tongue sticking to the roof of your mouth. (2) cheese except for Liederkranz, which has the same odour problem as tuna fish, and (3) certain Italian meats, but be careful with mortadella because it makes you burp."

"Maybe I'll just buy my lunch," Billy said.

"I support that idea."

Billy suddenly grew quiet and a worried look flickered across his face.

"What now?" Hoover said. "Don't tell me the loss of a tuna sandwich is going to make you cry?"

"I was just thinking that I hope I don't have to eat alone."

For the first time, the Hoove felt a twinge of

sympathy for this kid. No one, dead or alive, wants to eat alone on their first day at a new school.

"You won't have to eat alone," the Hoove said, "because I'm going to help you out here. Now, it all depends on how you enter the cafeteria. You want to be friendly, but not desperate. You're going to want to keep that Broccoli smile to a minimum. You smile so wide, radio waves bounce off your teeth."

Billy thought the Hoove actually had a point. He had spent the last eight years observing all the popular kids at his old school, and they had an easy way about them. No matter what was going on, they looked like nothing bothered them. When Billy struck out at baseball, he would go into his "strike-out slouch" and slither off the field, dragging his bat behind him. But when Adam Fox, the most popular kid in his year, struck out, he'd just glare back at the mound, as if the pitcher had done something wrong. It was all about attitude.

"So," the Hoove went on, "I want you to show me how you're going to enter the cafeteria. Go out into the hall and come back in with some of that Porterhouse swagger."

Billy picked up a world atlas from his desk and held it as if it were a tray. He went out into the hall and closed the door, where he encountered his stepfather, who was hanging some family photos on the wall.

"Excellent choice of reading material," Bennett said, noticing that Billy was carrying the atlas. "When I was your age, I could name the fifty longest rivers of the world *in alphabetical order* just from studying the atlas. Something to strive for, son."

"I'm going to get right on it, Bennett."

Billy quickly turned back to his bedroom door. He paused a moment to concentrate on being confident, then entered the room with his shoulders back and chin held high. Unfortunately, his chin was held so high that he didn't see his rucksack lying on the rug in front of him and he promptly tripped and hit the floor with a thump.

The Hoove attempted not to laugh. This kid was trying hard. It wasn't his fault that he was hopeless. Besides, Hoover never knew when the Higher-Ups were watching. Making fun of a worried kid who tripped over his own rucksack would certainly not raise his grade in Helping Others. But he couldn't stop himself. Watching Billy flail on the ground, trying to scamper to his feet while maintaining his cool, was truly funny. He let loose a tremendous laugh that echoed like a hollow screech on a Halloween sound-effects CD.

Billy was fuming mad.

"I'm trying my best here, man. And what I don't need is anybody laughing at me. I'm so nervous already that my armpits are practically squirting sweat and I haven't even left my room yet."

The Hoove stopped laughing. He heard the nervousness in Billy's voice, and he remembered how he had felt on his first day of junior high school. It had been ninety-nine years since he'd thought of that day, but when he let the memory in, he suddenly felt how hard it was to be eleven going on twelve. He drifted over to Billy and put his ghostly hand on his shoulder. Billy shivered and moved away. He was still angry about being laughed at.

"I don't need your sympathy," he said. "I can manage."

As Billy got to his feet, the Hoove reached out and took a baseball hat from the bed and popped it on Billy's head, giving it a jaunty twist to the side.

"Tell you what, sport," he said in his kindest voice. "Maybe I've given you too many rules for one day. So forget everything I said. Be yourself tomorrow, and you'll be great. Just do me one favour. DON'T TRIP."

That sounded easy enough, but Billy was so nervous, he wasn't even sure he could do that.

Chapter 6

The next morning, as Billy approached the main brick building of Moorepark Middle School, wearing his dark green T-shirt and jeans that were appropriately low on his waist, only one thought rolled around and around in his head.

"I will not trip," he thought. "Trip, I will not. This is me, not tripping. Never shall I trip."

Clusters of unfamiliar students stood around the flagpole, sat on the steps and hung out by the front door. Billy felt as if everyone was staring at him, judging him, checking out every detail about him. He wondered what they were thinking, if he measured up. He hoped that someone – anyone – would come up and say hello, or even toss him a welcoming nod. Just a crumb to make him feel like he belonged.

The Hoove had given him some tips on how to make a good first impression. "Just walk by, give them a confident nod, and snap your suspenders with both thumbs. Nothing says confidence like a suspender snap."

But of course that wasn't possible. Neither Billy nor anyone he had ever known wore suspenders. The Hoove had volunteered to get up early to check Billy out before he left, but when he found out that school started at seven forty-five in the morning, he announced to Billy that he didn't do mornings.

"Mornings are for roosters," he'd said. "And I do not cock-a-doodle-do."

Billy adjusted his rucksack, shoved his hands into his pockets, and stepped on to the school grounds. So far, so good. He walked up the concrete path, and when he reached the front steps, he noticed that a group of girls wearing navy blue school sports clothes seemed to be staring at him. He thought they were probably the cross-country team, and to show them how agile he was, he took the steps two at a time, putting a little bounce into each leap.

That was his first mistake.

The second was falling face down on the brick landing, just in front of the main entrance to school.

"I will not trip," he muttered to himself. "Change of plans. I just did."

He was more embarrassed than hurt. He couldn't bring himself to turn his head to see if the cross-country girls were laughing at him. As he looked up, a hand reached out to help him. Thank goodness, there was one kind person in this school.

"Hey, Broccoli, great three-point landing. Let me help you up."

It was Rod Brownstone, doing an unusually neighbourly thing.

"Thanks, Rod," Billy said, reaching out to grab Rod's hand. But Rod quickly withdrew his hand and left Billy lying on the ground, grasping at air.

"Just kidding, twinkle toes," Rod said. "But don't worry. I see two people who *aren't* laughing at you. Oh, wait, I'm wrong. They're laughing, too."

Billy wanted the ground to open so he could fall through and disappear. If he could, he would have stayed there, face down on the bricks, for the rest of the term. How could this be the first impression he was making at his new school? Was he doomed to be a dork for ever?

"Dude, they're going to charge you rent if you just keep lying there."

Billy looked up to see a large sixth grader, tall and muscular, looking down at him. The kid was wearing a Los Angeles Angels cap with a shock of thick black hair sticking out from under it. He extended his hand. Billy looked at him suspiciously, not knowing if this kid was going to pull a Rod Brownstone on him. But he didn't. The kid grabbed Billy's hand and, with one strong jerk, pulled him up to his feet.

"You going to need a stretcher?" he asked with a laugh.

"I'm OK," Billy answered. "Nothing that moving to another country can't cure."

"Ricardo Perez," the kid said.

"Billy Broccoli."

Billy waited for Ricardo to make fun of his name and say something like "Oh, I know your sister, Cheese Sauce" like most people did. But all Ricardo said was "Try keeping both feet on the pavement, dude. It makes walking easier."

Billy picked up his rucksack, brushed off his dust-covered T-shirt, and walked through the front entrance. His hands stung where he'd scraped them on the brick, but there was nothing to do about that now except pretend that everything was fine. Just fine.

"Are you OK, honey?"

Oh, no. It was his mother! Billy turned bright red with embarrassment as she came running out from the head teacher's office and took both of his hands in hers.

"I saw you trip from my office window," she said. "Let's get you to the nurse's office and clean those scrapes. She has something that doesn't sting."

Billy looked around the hall and noticed that the girls from the cross-country team were standing at their lockers, watching him. They looked surprised to see their head teacher holding hands with a student.

"Oh," Mrs Broccoli-Fielding laughed. "It's OK, girls. He's my son. Billy, have you met Ruby Baker and Tess Wu and Ava Daley . . . the pride of our cross-country team?"

Standing there holding hands with his mum, Billy thought of the Hoove and how horrified he would be by this pathetic scene.

"Mum," he whispered. "Now is not a good time to make new friends and influence people."

"Don't be silly, honey," his mum said. "People fall down all the time, don't they, girls?"

Two of the girls, the ones named Ava and Tess, just laughed. But the girl with the blonde ponytail – Ruby Baker – gave Billy an understanding smile.

"I'm a total klutz, too," she said. "In fact, last week I fell so hard during a practice that some of the track is permanently embedded in my knee."

"I know the feeling," Billy answered. "At my old school, I had a sliding accident at baseball practice. I've still got first base imprinted on my butt."

Ruby just stared at him.

Why am I discussing my backside with this girl I've just met? Billy thought. Immediately, he wished he could take back his words. But that was the trouble with words. Once they were out there, they just hung in the air for ever.

With as much dignity as he could muster, Billy removed his hands from his mother's grasp, nodded at the girls, and headed down the hall to his form room. The first person he saw when he entered his classroom was none other than Rod Brownstone. And just Billy's luck, the only seat available was next to him.

"Take a seat," Mr De Luca said. As Billy slid into his desk, he noticed Rod Brownstone staring him in the face.

"Hey, Broccoli," he said. "If you don't mind me calling you that. . ."

"Would it make any difference if I did?"

"Nope. So, Broccoli, tell me something. How come you talk to yourself in your room at night?"

"I don't know what you're referring to, Rod."

"I'm referring to last night, when I just happened to look through your window and saw you marching around your room, having a full conversation with yourself."

"What, are you spying on me?"

"I'm not spying. I'm gathering information. I'm the neighbourhood watch, didn't you know?"

"Really? Who appointed you?"

"I appointed myself. Somebody's got to step

up and keep track of the comings and goings on our street. You never know when there could be a 406 in progress."

"I can't wait for you to tell me what that is."

"Police code for breaking and entering," Rod snapped.

"Well, for your information, there was no 406 in progress in my room. Just a 282."

"Very funny, Broccoli. That number's not even in the code book."

"Yes, it is. It's in mine. It's code for *mind your own business*."

"Minding your business is my business," Rod whispered, getting his big, doughy face right up in Billy's. "I'm a citizen who takes the law very seriously. I bet you didn't know that, just last week, I reported someone on our block for a 586. The police were there in two and a half minutes and took corrective action."

"OK, I give up, Brownstone. What's a 586?"

"Illegal parking. Dark green Volkswagen hatchback."

Billy couldn't believe it. That was his grandmother's car.

"So you were the one who turned in my grandma?" he said.

"Had to, Broccoli. Her rear bumper was two fingers in the red."

"What a jerky thing to do, Brownstone. She came all the way from Santa Monica to let the gas man in. And then she had to spend the rest of the day getting her car out of the car pound, thanks to you. And that's not to mention the three hundred dollars it cost her."

Rod pretended he was playing the violin. "You're making me weep, Broccoli. And now you're starting to annoy me. This conversation is over."

That was fine with Billy. Seconds later, the bell rang and Mr De Luca called him to the front of the class to introduce himself and say a few words about his hobbies and interests. As Billy got up from his seat, the last thing he heard was Rod Brownstone whispering to him, "Remember this, Broccoli. I'm watching you."

Just to prove that he was a total, unmistakable, humongous jerk, Rod stuck out his foot as Billy passed by him, sending Billy stumbling down the row until he finally landed in a heap on the floor, right next to the desk occupied by Ruby Baker.

Billy looked up at her, and with the most confident, Hoove-inspired smile he could muster, said, "Nice to see you again."

Chapter 7

Hoover Porterhouse sat high up in the Birthday Tree, waiting for Billy to return from his first day of school. He liked to sit on the top branch so he could survey the comings and goings in the neighbourhood. Rod Brownstone had arrived home from school an hour earlier, taken his rucksack into the house, and returned to the back garden with a short-wave radio on which he was following the local police report. It was a slow afternoon for Rod since no one in the neighbourhood had been arrested or had even double-parked. Rod's little sister, Amber, stood on the seat of a swing that hung from the apricot tree in their garden. She was trying to learn how to swing standing up, even though her mother had told her not to do that.

Over at the Broccoli–Fielding house, Breeze was busy in the basement, auditioning girls to replace the bass player in her band, the Dark Cloud. The thumping sounds of five girls playing the bass all at once streamed out of the basement window and hung in the air around the Hoove's tree. He covered his ears to block out the sound, but it didn't do any good because his hands had no matter to them. That's the way it was with ghost hands. They just didn't matter.

Dr Fielding had come home early and was getting the barbecue ready for the flank steak that was marinating in the kitchen. Mrs Broccoli–Fielding sat at the picnic table outside and kept her husband company while she looked over the day's attendance records.

The only person not in evidence was Billy. The Hoove wondered what had happened to the kid. Whatever it was, he had a feeling it wasn't good. He scanned the horizon in all directions, but all he could see was Mrs Pearson riding on her electric lawn mower around her corner lawn. Her rear didn't quite fit on the seat. *Mrs Pearson must enjoy her own cooking*, he thought.

Then something caught his eye. Someone was darting from tree to tree, from parked car to parked car, like a squirrel being chased by the neighbourhood dog. But squirrels didn't wear dark green T-shirts or sweatshirts with the hood pulled up around their heads.

It was Billy Broccoli, hiding so that he could avoid a human encounter of any kind. The day had been rough for him, and he didn't want to embarrass himself one more time. He had reached the bottom of his embarrassment well and realized it was dry as a bone. Seeing that no one was on the street, he slipped out from behind the sycamore and made a run for the house. He didn't like what he saw. All he wanted was to be alone, to slip into his room, close the door, and end the day. But instead, it seemed like everyone he knew was outside waiting to greet him.

"Howdy, son," Dr Fielding said, wiping a smudge of grill grease off his forehead. "Have a seat and tell us all about your first day. Don't skip one detail."

"Thanks, Bennett, but I've got some important business to take care of." And then, lowering his voice to a whisper, Billy added, "You know . . . the men's room."

"Oh, gotcha," Bennett whispered back. "When a man's gotta go, a man's gotta go."

Bennett held up his hand for a high five, and Billy wondered what was possibly so bonding about sharing that he had to pee. But Bennett was a nice man, and Billy returned his high five before hurrying into the house.

His eyes were so focused on the door to his room that he didn't notice the girl walking up the stairs from the basement until he ran smack into her.

"Oh, sorry," he started to say, until he realized it was Ruby Baker, the girl with the bouncing blonde ponytail who had witnessed not one, but two of the most embarrassing moments of his entire life. Billy realized that this was a perfect opportunity to create a different impression on her, and he racked his brain for something to say. Ruby beat him to it.

"I bet you're wondering what I'm doing here," she said.

Billy tried to answer, but his brain turned immediately to cream cheese. Luckily, Ruby was so comfortable in her own skin, she didn't need an answer.

"My sister Sofia is auditioning for your sister's band. She's a bass player. My mum made me come along because she doesn't want me to stay alone in the house. And Sofia sent me up here to get her rucksack from your kitchen."

Ruby paused and waited for an answer. Billy opened his mouth, but what came out sounded something like "Oooo . . . uhhhh . . . uhhhh . . . eeeuuu . . . oooo . . . ummm."

"Spit it out, ducky."

Billy tried to locate the voice but couldn't.

"Up here, Billy Boy."

Billy looked up to see Hoover Porterhouse floating on the ceiling above Ruby's head.

"You sound like a train stalled on the tracks. Give it some steam, my friend."

"Don't push me," Billy whispered. "I'm trying."

"Try faster. Your potential new friend is waiting. She's not going to stand there for ever."

Turning to Ruby, Billy said the first thing that popped into his head, "I bet you barely recognized me standing up." He tried to sound light and breezy. It must have worked because Ruby laughed.

"Yeah, you seem to have had a little trouble with your feet today."

"I'm going to go ahead and blame that on my

shoes," Billy answered. "They've got a mind of their own."

"Maybe you should wear different shoes tomorrow."

Billy tried to come up with a funny answer to that, but his brain returned to its former cream-cheese state. After an awkward silence, Ruby went into the kitchen, got her sister's rucksack, and went back down to the basement, where the bass guitars were still thumping out the beat.

"Well, that was a start," the Hoove commented, drifting down from the ceiling and hovering at Billy's eye level. "You almost got a conversation going except you kind of petered out at the end."

"I'm shy with new people, and that pressure from you didn't help."

Billy turned on his heel and stomped off to his bedroom, slamming the door behind him. But a closed door was no barrier for Hoover Porterhouse, who zipped into Billy's room straight after him.

"It is not my fault you ran out of steam," he said. "You just stood there like a statue while your tongue went on holiday to Argentina."

"I was just trying to think of something funny to say."

"Well, here's what it looked like from the ceiling. It looked like you were either going to throw up all over your shoes or pass out. Either move would have been highly unacceptable to the lady in question."

"You don't understand what happened between me and her today at school."

"Please make it an appetizing story."

"I tripped going up the front steps. And she was watching."

"Tripped? What was the last thing I told you before you left this abode?"

"I know. Do you think I had a plan to trip? It just happened. Look, I even scraped up my hands."

Billy held his hands up in front of the Hoove, who suddenly turned even paler than he already was.

"Don't show me that. Skin that is not attached to a person makes my blood curdle. Or it would, if I had blood."

"Well, I'm not thrilled about the situation either. You can't believe how my hands hurt when I went to baseball tryouts after school. I could barely hold the bat. And when I was fielding, the palms of my hands stung every time the ball came to me."

The Hoove, who had flopped himself down on Billy's bed, suddenly popped to his feet and glided over right next to Billy's face.

"Wait a minute," he said, looking outraged. "You went to baseball tryouts and you didn't tell me?"

"Since when are you in charge of my schedule? And please, would you back off? You smell like a sack of sour oranges."

"It happens when I get upset. My scent can get a little tart. But don't try to change the subject. Did you make the team, is what I want to know."

"As a matter of fact, I did."

"Atta boy. What position? Catcher? Naw, a scrawny kid like you would never be a catcher. So what are you, centre field? Second base? Shortstop? Speak up."

"You're looking at the new assistant scorekeeper of the junior varsity baseball team at Moorepark Middle School," Billy announced with some pride.

"So what does that mean? You work your way up to head scorekeeper?"

"No, they don't have that position."

"Billy Boy, let me shed some light on this situation for you," the Hoove said. "What you're telling me is that you get no playing time. You are going to sit on the bench and keep score. Your hands are never going to touch a ball or a glove."

"The coach didn't say that."

"Trust me, he was thinking it."

Hoover paced back and forth in the way that ghosts pace, which is to say, there was no pacing involved. He just floated back and forth across the room at an accelerated rate.

"I don't know why you didn't consult with me, Billy. You happen to be looking at the batting champion of the San Fernando Junior Cougars. They say I was headed for the majors. I know a thing or two about baseball. Show me your stance."

Billy reluctantly picked up one of the aluminium bats that was propped up in the corner of his room and assumed his best batting stance.

"No wonder you weren't chosen," the Hoove said, casting a disapproving eye at Billy. "Look at you. Plant your feet further apart. Sit into the stance. Put your hands together on the bat. And get your elbow down. You look like you're some kind of poultry, flapping your wings for a take off."

Billy tried to make each adjustment as Hoover called out instructions. He was so busy concentrating on keeping his elbow down and his bottom in that he didn't notice the figure standing at his bedroom door.

It was Rod Brownstone.

"You have to be the weirdest dude that's ever lived here," he said. "Do you make a habit of talking to yourself?"

"Do you make a habit of barging into people's rooms without even being invited?" Billy responded. "People you hardly know?"

"I brought over a pineapple upside-down cake my mum made for your family," Rod explained. "And your mum said I should come in and establish a relationship with you. That's a quote."

"That sounds like my mum, all right."

"I didn't want to come because I make it a point not to hang out with assistant score-keepers who don't have an ice cube's chance in the desert of being a ballplayer."

"For you information, Brownstone, I'm working on my batting stance with a private coach who was almost in the majors."

"Really? Well, did your coach notice that those toothpicks you call arms don't have enough muscle to hold a bat? Not like these guns." Rod held up his arms, flexed his biceps, and kissed them both. Billy looked at his own meagre biceps and decided no kissing was called for.

Rod's arrogance infuriated the Hoove. He was not about to let this blowbag insult Billy. The Hoove was actually surprised that he cared so much.

"Billy Broccoli, you cannot let him get away with that," he said, his voice full of anger. "Answer him."

But Billy just stood there feeling helpless. Deep down, he knew Rod was probably right. Being the assistant scorekeeper of the baseball team was almost like not being on the team at all.

Hoover couldn't stand it. He wanted to protect Billy from this big-mouthed kid. And that really surprised him, since in all his ninety-nine years of being a ghost, he had never felt this way about any of the other kids he had been assigned. What he really wanted to do was punch Rod in the nose, but if he did that, Rod would punch Billy. Besides, the Higher-Ups did not look kindly on physical violence of any kind. So he had to move to Plan B, which was to scare Rod into a quivering clump of jelly.

He started with the always reliable spinning-picture trick. He reached out and took the corner of the framed Dodgers poster hanging on Billy's wall and spun it so that it twirled like a top on the wall. Then he just smiled for a second while he watched Rod's eyes start to grow wider.

"How did you do that?" Rod asked Billy.

The Hoove knew the fun had just begun. He floated over to Billy's desk and lifted it several centimetres off the ground, then made it shake violently in mid-air.

"Do you see that desk vibrating?" Rod asked, his voice cracking.

Billy was starting to enjoy this.

"I don't see anything," he said. "What are you talking about?"

"Don't mess with me, Broccoli. I know you see what I see. How are you making that happen?"

"I'm standing right here in front of you," Billy said. "Doing nothing."

"Well, then, you are an alien," Rod said. "I've always known this house had a weird vibe, but I've never seen anything this strange. It's almost as strange as you. I'm out of here, and by the way, don't invite me back. You and your room creep me out."

"First of all," Billy said, "I didn't invite you. And second of all, don't let the door hit you on the way out."

Rod was in such a rush to get out of there, he pulled a Hoove. He tried to walk through the door without opening it, and smacked his forehead right into it. Furious, he flung the door open and tore down the hall without looking back.

Billy burst out laughing, and so did the Hoove. They could hardly contain themselves, as each did their own impression of Rod trying to get out of the room. *Thunk! Bang! Slap!* Billy was practically crying with laughter. As he and the Hoove replayed the image of Rod Brownstone thumping into the door and then tearing down the hall almost peeing in his pants with fear, Billy thought for the first time that maybe having your own personal ghost could be useful after all.

Chapter 8

Rod Brownstone was in a panic as he sprinted out of Billy's room. He wasn't the kind of guy who showed fear easily, but whatever had happened in that bedroom had rattled his ever-confident cover. As he reached the kitchen, he spotted Ruby, Sofia and Breeze coming up from the basement, and screeched to a full stop just before crashing into them.

"Hey, ladies," he said, trying to recover as best he could. He tried desperately to appear calm and self-assured, but he must not have been too convincing because Breeze took one look at him and asked, "Are you all right?"

"Sure." He shrugged. "I mean, why wouldn't I be? What could possibly be wrong? I can't think of one thing. I was just hanging out with your brother."

Ruby smiled. "Billy?" she said. "He's cute, in his own trippy kind of way."

"Yeah, you could say that if you think dorks are cute, that is," Rod shot back.

He didn't like it one bit that Ruby had said something nice about Billy. He always thought every girl had a secret crush on him, and it offended him that Ruby Baker didn't seem to be joining the club. Besides, what could she possibly see in Billy Broccoli that she didn't see in him? He certainly did not want to hear anything positive about that little squirt. Somewhere in the back of his mind, a thought began to hatch – a thought that he was going to change Ruby's opinion of Billy Broccoli.

He decided to start right then and there with a list of everything that was wrong with Billy, beginning with his short stature and moving on to his clumsy feet. But before he could get out a full sentence, Sofia interrupted him.

"Ruby, we have to go," she said. "Mum said we have to be home by five o'clock, which was ten minutes ago. Sorry to play and run, Breeze."

"That's OK," Breeze answered. "Now that you're in the band, we'll have lots of time to hang out when we rehearse."

Sofia and Ruby said goodbye to Breeze, leaving Rod standing there feeling frustrated that he hadn't got Ruby to fall madly in love with him.

"Who's in the mood for flank steak?" Dr Fielding asked as he came into the kitchen to get the meat out of the refrigerator.

"Me," Breeze answered. "I'm starving."

"I thought you were a vegetarian, sweetie."

"That was yesterday, Dad."

"Oh, I see. Well, the fire's all ready. I just came in here to get the steaks."

"I guess I should go, then," Rod said. "I don't want to interrupt your dinnertime."

"Nonsense, young Rod." Bennett put a hand on his shoulder and gave him the comforting squeeze he had perfected in his years of being a dentist. "You're welcome to stay. There's plenty of food. Billy isn't much of a meat eater."

"His favourite food is crisp sandwiches," Breeze said. "Oh, and he likes to eat olives off the tips of his fingers. He's what you call majorly weird. And let's not forget the tonsil."

"He eats tonsils?" Rod asked.

"Not that I know of," Breeze said. "But I wouldn't put it past him. He keeps his own tonsil in a jar under his bed. Yesterday, he actually tried to display it on the shelf in the bathroom we share, but I said, 'No way, José... I'm not putting on my make-up staring at something that used to be in your throat.'"

"How old is that tonsil?" Rod asked.

"Beats me. Five years old. Maybe seven."

"I believe Charlotte mentioned Billy had his tonsils removed when he was six," Dr Fielding said. "That would make it five years old. It's almost ready to start school." He laughed heartily at his own joke.

"It must look gross," Rod said.

"The human body isn't gross, Rod," Dr Fielding said. "It's fascinating. Now, if there were still pus on the tonsil, I could understand your reaction. But the tonsil itself is just a ball of tissue made up of blood and cells and protoplasm. Not entirely different from the steaks we're having for dinner."

"Eeuuwww, Dad," Breeze said. "I think I just became a vegetarian again."

"Rod, why don't you call your mother and ask if you can stay for dinner," Dr Fielding said as he headed towards the back door with the plate of steaks. "And, Breeze, get Billy and tell him the food will be on the table in seven minutes. . . Three and half minutes per side is my secret for medium rare perfection."

On his way out, Dr Fielding grabbed a long two-pronged fork that he used for flipping the meat, and a timer that was set for exactly seven minutes. Breeze reached into her jeans pocket and pulled out her mobile phone.

"You can use my phone," she said to Rod, "while I go grab the little one."

"There's no point in calling. My mum's at work until seven. And my dad's taking Amber to Indian Princesses, so I'm fine for a while. Besides, I really want to check out your brother's tonsil."

"Suit yourself," Breeze said. "But I'm warning you. You're going to be grossed out."

As Rod followed Breeze down the hall, he decided to bring up the subject that was bothering him. "Hey, Breeze," he began. "Have you ever noticed anything strange going on in Billy's room?"

"Yeah, only like every minute he's in there. Don't forget, this is the boy who draws bolts of lightning on his feet with a Sharpie."

"I mean anything *really* strange, like, say, pictures spinning or furniture moving?"

Breeze stopped abruptly and turned to stare at Rod. "*Now* who's acting strange?"

Rod shut up fast.

Breeze knocked on Billy's door and, as usual, entered before she was even finished knocking. Billy was sitting at his desk with his maths book open, copying some problems on to a sheet of notebook paper. His calculator was out although he hardly ever needed to use it. Maths was his best subject and he could do most calculations in his head. He was surprised to see Breeze, and even more surprised to see that Rod was back. Billy knew that if the Hoove were still there, he'd have scared Rod away again, but the Hoove was gone, having left the premises as soon as Billy started his homework. The Hoove said he was allergic to homework. He said it gave him a rash, which Billy didn't exactly understand. Hoover had no skin, so what exactly did the rash appear on? But the Hoove was not interested in Billy's logic, and simply floated out through the window, saying he'd be back when he'd be back.

"Dad says dinner is in seven minutes," Breeze announced.

"We're having steak," Rod added.

"*We?*"

"Yeah, your stepdad invited me for dinner. I think he likes me, but then, who doesn't? I'm used to being admired. Like that girl Ruby who was here. She's a fan. I can just feel it."

"Right, Brownstone," Billy snarled. "Everyone loves you. According to you, that is."

"You got that right," Rod said, pushing his way further into Billy's room. "Hey, dude, if it's OK with you, I was hoping to get a look at that tonsil you keep in a jar."

Billy jumped to his feet and stared at Breeze.

"You . . . you . . . you told him about my tonsil?" he stammered. "I thought we had a pact."

"It slipped out, Billy. Honest. I didn't mean to say it."

"Fine, then watch this slip out." Billy turned to Rod. "You know that high school guy who drives the red—"

Breeze pounced on Billy like a tiger. "Don't you dare tell!"

"I won't tell," Billy said, removing her hand

from over his mouth. "Because unlike some people I know, I keep my word."

While Billy and Breeze argued about which secrets they would or would not spill, Rod took the opportunity to casually glance around the room for the tonsil. He thought he spotted it under the bed, just where Breeze said Billy kept it. Trying to look completely natural, Rod inched his way across the room, stuck his foot under the bed, and slid the jar out into the open. He bent down, picked it up, and held it up to the light to inspect its contents.

It wasn't a pretty sight. The fluid in which the tonsil lived was murky, the colour of old fish-tank water. And the tonsil itself had a long, fleshy string trailing behind it, like a half-rotten tail. Every now and then, when Rod rotated the jar, the tonsil would turn on its side and bounce off the side of the glass.

"Wow, this is worse than I could have ever imagined," Rod said. "I bet it stinks, too. You don't ever take the lid off, do you?"

Billy shot across the room and grabbed the jar out of Rod's hands.

"Give me that!" he shouted. "It's a little piece of me, and it's not available for public inspection!"

"Fine, you can have it. It's disgusting," Rod said. "Like the rest of you."

Holding the jar tightly to make sure it was secure, Billy returned to his desk, where Breeze was still standing.

"Eeuuuwww!" she screamed. "Get that thing out of my sight before I totally gag."

"Do what she says, you freak," Rod chimed in.

Billy pulled open the top drawer of his desk, put the jar inside, and shoved it all the way to the back.

"There, you satisfied?" he said.

As he closed the drawer, Mrs Broccoli-Fielding called from the kitchen.

"Dinner's ready!" she hollered. "Grab your own drink from the fridge on the way out."

"Finally," Breeze said. "Come on, guys. My dad makes great steaks."

"What are you going to have?" Rod said to Billy. "Barbecued tonsil?"

He let out one of his spit-spraying laughs, which Billy ignored as he followed Breeze into the hall. Rod Brownstone started after them, then stopped suddenly, as an idea entered his thick skull. They didn't enter very often, and when they did, they were usually half-baked, but Rod happened to think this one had a certain brilliance to it.

"I'll be right there," he called. "Just have to tie my shoe."

As soon as Billy and Breeze were out of sight, Rod quickly took off his checked shirt, opened the desk drawer, and removed the tonsil jar, wrapping it in his shirt so no one could tell it was there. Then he smiled a devilish smile, tucked the shirt under his arm, and left Billy's room with a bounce in his step.

Chapter 9

"All right, let's go over the procedures one more time," Hoover said to Billy.

It was the next morning, and the Hoove was giving Billy some last-minute instructions for his second day of school. He wanted to make sure there was no repeat of the previous day's disaster. Billy stuffed his books and papers into his rucksack, listening to the Hoove with only one ear. Maybe even half an ear.

"Billy Boy, are you listening to me? I don't see you paying attention."

Billy was concentrating on the zip of his rucksack, which had got stuck on the pages of his maths homework. "I got it, Hoove. Hoove's

Rule Number Forty-seven: 'No onions for breakfast, grilled or otherwise'."

"You see that," the Hoove said. "All my effort is for naught. I moved on from that five minutes ago. If you had been paying attention, you'd know that what I am discussing with you now is Rule Number Three, also known as the Nod."

"Right," Billy said. "The Nod."

"Now observe. I will demonstrate."

The Hoove floated off Billy's desk and strutted dramatically across the rug, snapping his suspenders when he arrived at the other side of the room.

"This is how you do it, Billy Boy. Notice the confidence, the powerful aura."

"Excuse me, Hoove. Do you remember who you're talking to? I don't have a pinky finger full of confidence, let alone a powerful aura."

"All the more reason for you to study what I'm doing. This is for your future, ducky. Now for the Nod. You walk up the front steps, and as you reach the top, you nod ever so slightly. But only to those who nod at you first. Try it. Let me see your best nod."

Billy put down his rucksack with a sigh and strutted across the room, trying to imitate the Hoove, but on him it looked less like a swagger and more like a chicken trying to climb out of a puddle.

"Now nod," the Hoove commanded.

Billy looked out at an imaginary group of students and, instead of nodding, started to wave his hand enthusiastically.

"Hold it! Hold it right there! Who said anything about waving? There is no waving involved here. How did you get from nodding your head to flapping your hand?"

"In my mind, I was happy to see everyone," Billy said. "I saw them all smiling."

A hopeless feeling swept over Hoover. This kid was proving to be really difficult. He had no instinct for cool. In fact, Billy just naturally went in the totally opposite direction.

"Listen to me," the Hoove instructed. "What

the Nod says is 'I'm happy to see you and you're lucky because of it.' This is all communicated with just the smallest move of your head."

"What's wrong with waving?"

"The wave moves you from acceptable to dorkdom. Don't question what I say. Just know that it's true. I've had ninety-nine years to perfect the Nod."

Billy slung his rucksack over his shoulder and headed for the door.

"I wish I could go with you today," the Hoove said. "You need some serious coaching."

"Well, I'm glad you can't. If you think waving is weird, can you imagine how everyone would react if I showed up with a ghost? Oh yeah, there's nothing weird about that."

After a quick breakfast of shredded wheat and milk, Billy set off for school. He felt good about the fact that Breeze allowed him to walk with her. It was unusual for a sixth grader to walk to school with a seventh grader, especially with one who had her own band and tons of friends at Moorepark. He tried to match her confidence, and began to strut in the most Hoover-like way he could.

"Did your jeans shrink in the wash or something?" Breeze asked him as they rounded the corner of their block and headed up Moorepark Avenue.

"No. Why?"

"You're walking funny. Like you have a giant wedgie."

Billy decided that maybe the strut wasn't for him, and he resumed his normal gait, which was like a pony learning to trot. He had always been small, and he found it easiest to keep up if he trotted.

When Billy and Breeze reached school, Breeze was immediately surrounded by her friends, who led her off to get hot chocolate at the cafeteria, leaving Billy alone at the foot of the steps.

"Don't trip," he said to himself as he walked up the stairs.

And he didn't.

That was good. The day was already off to a much better start than his miserable first day. As he walked in the front door, Billy passed Ricardo Perez, who was getting a drink of water. Ricardo nodded to him, and Billy gave him a Hoove-style nod back. It must have worked, because Ricardo actually spoke to him.

"Look who's here. The new assistant scorekeeper. Got your pencils sharpened?"

"It's kind of a drag," Billy answered. "I was hoping to play."

"You have to show Coach you're developing your skills. The last scorekeeper eventually made the team. Never got a hit, but he learned to spit sunflower shells further than anybody else."

"Thanks, Ricardo. You're a pal. I really appreciate the encouragement."

"Here's a tip, dude. Get yourself a pack of sunflower seeds and start practising."

Billy was amazed at how nice this guy was. So

far, his day had been perfect. The opposite of the day before. Maybe his mother was right when she said that it was just a matter of time until he'd feel right at home in his new school.

Billy's morning classes couldn't have gone smoother. In maths, Mr Bentley asked him to go to the board and solve a problem, and not only did he get it right, he noticed that Ruby Baker seemed to be impressed with his mathematical skills. She didn't say that outright, of course, but he thought he noticed her smiling at him for a split second as he headed back to his seat.

After class, when he stopped by his new locker to put his books away, he was able to open the combination on the first try. It seemed like everything was falling into place.

Even at lunch, he didn't have to sit by himself. Ricardo and a couple of the guys from the baseball team hadn't objected when he sat at their table. His seat was at the very end of the table, but still, that was a lot better than sitting by himself.

As he sat in the outside lunch pavillion, the warm California sun beaming down on him, Billy unwrapped his peanut butter, jam and crisp sandwich with a sense of well-being that was entirely new to him. To make the day even better, Ruby Baker and several of the cross-country girls had stopped at Billy's table on their way out of the salad bar line. There they all were, talking and laughing.

Billy Broccoli . . . part of the group. Man, that felt good.

He was so busy having a great time that Billy didn't notice Rod leaving the football team table and tucking his checked shirt under one arm. Rod walked over to where Ruby and her friends always sat, looked stealthily around, then unfolded the shirt and took out the glass jar with Billy's tonsil in it. That morning, he'd attached a note to it that said: *Dear Ruby. Here is a little piece of me. Want to join my tonsil and me for lunch? Love, Billy Broccoli.*

Quickly, Rod placed the tonsil jar and the

note on the table in front of Ruby's usual seat and rejoined his football friends.

Ruby and the girls continued to chat with the boys for a few more minutes, then carried their trays to their own table and sat down. Billy turned back to the conversation with the baseball team, when suddenly—

"Eeeuuuwwwwwwww!" It was Ruby, screaming at the top of her lungs. "What is that? Get it out of here!"

Everyone in the lunch pavillion stopped what they were doing and looked at Ruby. She hopped up from the table and danced around like her feet were on fire.

"Eeeuuwwwwwww!" she screamed again. Then all the girls at her table joined in. "Eeeuuwww, eeeuuwww, triple eeeuuwwww!" they shrieked.

Every pair of eyes in the lunch area was focused on Ruby. No one knew exactly what had happened, except that something extremely eeeuuuwww-y had transpired.

"This is so not funny, Billy Broccoli," she

said, marching directly over to him. "I don't want to have lunch with you or with that thing in the jar."

Billy just sat there with his mouth open, his peanut butter, jam and crisp sandwich suspended in mid-air. He had no idea what had just happened. Meanwhile, at the football table, Rod Brownstone was having himself the laugh of the century.

A bunch of kids had clustered around Ruby's table to see what was in the jar that had her so freaked out. Billy's tonsil lay there at the bottom, suspended in its murky goo, looking in the daylight even more stringy and fleshy than usual.

"Check it out!" Sammy Park hooted. "It's even got a label. 'Billy's tonsil. Removed at Sherman Oaks Hospital, 7 April, 10:00 a.m.'"

"Oooohhhhhhhh, gross."

It seemed like everyone in the lunch area was saying it at once. Billy was humiliated, ashamed and angry beyond words. He jumped to his feet and charged towards Ruby's table, where Sammy Park was holding his tonsil up to the sun and shaking it to make it wiggle.

"That's mine!" he said, grabbing the jar.

He immediately wished he could take that back. How could he have confessed in front of everyone that this was his tonsil?

With a mighty rush of nervous energy, he tucked the tonsil jar under his arm and bolted out of the lunch area. He ran as fast as he could. But where could he go? There was nowhere he could escape the awful embarrassment that filled his body from head to toe.

The last thing he saw as he left the pavillion was Rod Brownstone, fist-bumping his friends, taking full credit for the worst moment of Billy's life.

Chapter 10

Hoover Porterhouse was actually doing homework, which was almost unheard of in all his ninety-nine years of ghostly existence. Hanging around Billy's room, with all its baseball gear piled up in the corner, had made him remember how much he missed the game and how much he longed to see the baseball fields of America. He knew he was never going to get there unless he brought up his grades. And although he was a procrastinator of the first degree, he had managed to fire himself up enough to work on one subject... Invisibility.

Hoover's invisibility skills were inconsistent at best. To practice, he had forced himself to hang out at the Birthday Tree and whistle "I've Been Working on the Railroad" for two solid hours. At first, he thought he saw improvement, but the last couple of times he tried it, only his feet appeared. Hoover had been told by an older ghost, Bernie Highwater, who haunted the hardware store next to the cinema, that invisibility was a matter of concentration. According to Bernie, the very act of whistling cleared your mind enough so that you could fully concentrate on making yourself visible.

It was that state of mind that Hoover was looking for.

He had been whistling that same stupid song for most of the afternoon and was getting really sick of it and frustrated that only his boots were standing by themselves on the leafy ground under the tree. Occasionally, a knee popped up, but that was as far as he could get, visibility-wise. Hoover wasn't sure how much more whistling he could do. His mouth felt like it was full of cotton balls. He was actually relieved to see Billy Broccoli coming home from school. Throwing himself into Swoosh mode, he rushed across the garden so he could beat Billy to the back door.

"Welcome home," he said, holding the screen door open.

Billy looked at the Hoove, or at least the parts of Hoove that were visible, and jumped nearly a metre in the air.

"You're kidding me," the Hoove said. "I still scare you?"

"If you had big things on your mind and suddenly you were approached by a pair of boots and one knee, I think you'd jump, too."

Billy pushed past the Hoove, or at least what was visible of the Hoove, walked into the kitchen, and yanked open the fridge, pulling the door so hard it made all the salad-dressing bottles clatter. He took out a bowl of leftover potato salad, took a clean fork out of the dishwasher, and started to shovel the food into his mouth without even remembering that he hated potato salad. Something about the crunch of the celery next to the mush of the potatoes repulsed him.

"This is anger eating," the Hoove said to Billy. "And it's unattractive on any human, living or dead."

"Yeah, well, so is having one knee."

"I'm working on that. In the meantime, why don't you spill the beans. I can tell, something is very wrong."

"Wrong? What could possibly be wrong?" Billy answered, exposing some mildly disgusting clumps of potato salad on his tongue. "Just because everybody at school thinks I'm a total freak for keeping my tonsil in a jar? What's wrong with that?"

"Are you telling me you took that disgusto fleshy thing to school?" Hoover asked. "Has your mind left the building?"

"Of course I didn't take it. Rod Brownstone swiped it last night and put it on the lunch table right in front of Ruby and everyone else I might ever want to be friends with but now never will be."

"Brownstone? That twit?"

"The very same."

"He did that to you? I can't believe it! This is totally unacceptable."

"Tell me about it."

The Hoove felt a rush of anger swell up in him.

"I never liked that twerp," he fumed. "He's a bad egg inside and out. But now he has crossed the Hoove's line. I'm telling you, Billy, and hear me well: anyone who messes with you, messes with me. Big-time."

Suddenly, right in front of Billy's eyes, the Hoove appeared, his whole body totally visible, newsboy cap, suspenders and all.

"Whoa," he said. "I've been working on that all day. Thank you, Billy Boy. You and your Rod story focused me, and lo and behold, here I am in my full greatness."

"Good for you," Billy said, reaching for the

milk and taking a swig right out of the bottle. "Your life ... or whatever you call it ... is fabulous. Mine is ruined. So if you'll pardon me, I'm going to my room to hide in the wardrobe for the next twenty years. It's been nice knowing you."

"OK, but you might want to wipe that egg salad off your face before it forms a crust."

"It's potato salad."

"Whatever it is, it should not be on your face. It should be on a napkin, which should be placed immediately at the bottom of the rubbish bin."

The Hoove laughed to lighten the mood, but Billy's spirits couldn't be lifted.

"What is that?" he snapped. "Hoove's Rule One Thousand and Ten? You know what, Hoove? I've had it with your rules and with your advice. There's nothing that's going to help me now. My life as I've known it is over. From now on, I'm just going to be known as the pathetic guy who keeps body parts as souvenirs."

Billy didn't even bother to put the potato salad or the milk back in the fridge. What did it matter if his mum got mad at him for messing up the kitchen? What did anything matter now? Without another word, he turned and left, stomping down the hall to his room and slamming the door behind him.

The Hoove did some serious stomping of his own. Without hesitation, he stomped out of the house, stomped across the garden, and stomped directly into the Brownstone house. Once inside, he threw himself into hyperglide, swooping around their house, looking for the Brownstone twerp. He swept past Amber, who sat at the kitchen table, colouring dresses in her princess colouring book. He was moving so fast that the pages in her book actually flapped in the gust of wind he created. Amber looked up to see if anyone was there, and when she didn't see anyone, she yelled, "Mummy, I'm not alone, but I don't see anybody." Her mother came in from the utility room, looked around, and gave Amber a little kiss on the forehead.

"You have such an active imagination, honey," she said. "You could be a writer when you grow up."

Rod was sitting in the living room, doing his perfect imitation of a couch potato. He held the TV remote in one hand and a bag of flaming-hot spicy nacho crisps in the other. He was staring at the fourth rerun of an episode of *Unsolved Parking Tickets*, the one about a cross-eyed guy whose parking meter ran out seven years ago. It was just his kind of entertainment.

The moment the Hoove spotted him, he zoomed over to the television and flicked it off.

"Hey," Rod grunted, and flicked the TV back on with the remote.

It wasn't back on for a second when the Hoove pulled the plug out. Brownstone sat there clicking the remote over and over, but of course, the TV did not go on.

"Who keeps messing with the TV in here?" he shouted to no one in particular.

When the big lug got up to see what was wrong with the TV, the Hoove zipped over to the bag of crisps lying on the coffee table. He picked it up and, with an impish grin, dumped its contents out. When Rod turned around, he saw his favourite crisps strewn all over the rug, and their bulldog, Rambo, happily scarfing them down.

"What's going on in here?" Rod said to himself.

"I'm just getting warmed up," the Hoove bellowed, even though Rod couldn't hear him. "I'm going to teach you never to mess around with my buddy Billy Broccoli."

Just then, Mrs Brownstone happened to walk into the living room on her way to put Rod's clean laundry on his bed. When she saw the mess on the carpet, her face turned bright red. She kept a very tidy house, and the sight of crushed crisps and dog slobber on her new carpet did not sit well with her.

"Rodney Richard Brownstone, you know the rules about eating in the living room. Go get the hand vacuum right now and put it to good use."

"Mum, I'm right in the middle of my favourite show."

"No, you're right in the middle of my living room, and you're going to clean it up immediately."

Rod made a face at his mother, but she didn't see it because she was already heading to his bedroom. Angrily, he marched into the kitchen, where the hand vac hung on a hook next to the fridge, along with the brooms and a dustpan. The Hoove was right on his tail. As Rod reached for the hand vac, the Hoove reached for the broom and, assuming his best baseball stance, swatted Rod directly on his behind. Rod wheeled around and saw Amber sitting at the table, with the broom lying on the floor next to her.

"What's the big idea?" he yelled at her.

She shrugged. "I don't know what you're

talking about. And stop screaming. People do not yell at princesses."

"I can scream all I want. You just hit me with the broom!"

"I did not. You threw the broom over here at me."

"You're lying."

"No, you're the liar."

Hoover was pleased to see the argument grow. Getting under Rod's skin was the most fun he'd had since 1988, when he watched the World Series on TV and saw Kirk Gibson hit a home run for the Dodgers. He must have watched the reruns of that five hundred times.

"I'm going to tell Mum on you," Amber was saying. "You're going to be grounded until for ever."

Hoover didn't think being grounded for ever was long enough for Rod Brownstone. He didn't feel even a little bit bad for him, just as Rod hadn't felt bad about being so mean to Billy. The Hoove's Rule Number Sixty-Two was "The energy you put out is the energy you get back."

Getting Rod in trouble at home was amusing, but it didn't totally satisfy the Hoove. It didn't fix what Rod had done to Billy. Taking that tonsil to school was such a bully thing to do, and if there was one thing Hoover Porterhouse did not tolerate, it was a bully.

Back when he was alive, there was a kid named Clive McGraw who always used to pick on Sally Huerta, who was born with one leg a little shorter than the other. She wore a special shoe with a thick sole so she'd be able to walk like the other kids. But Clive used to make fun of her and imitate the way she ran. Some of the other kids would laugh at his antics, but never Hoover Porterhouse. In fact, he made it a point to strike out Clive McGraw every time that bully came up to bat. Eventually, he confronted Clive.

"What is your problem?" he had said to Clive. "What exactly does Sally do to you that is so terrible? I want you to look me square in the eye and tell my why you enjoy picking on that girl. Come on, let's see how tough you really are."

Clive couldn't come up with any answer, not even a syllable. After that conversation, Clive stopped bothering Sally, and eleven years later, after Hoove had been dead for a good decade, Sally and Clive wound up as husband and wife. As a ghost, the Hoove had always felt proud of his role in their destiny.

The Hoove watched with pleasure as Rod stomped into the living room and started vacuuming up the mess he'd made. He held the hand vac to the spot on the rug where the crisps had crumbled into the shag of the carpet. Rod hated cleaning. He hated the dust that was shooting up his nose. He hated losing all his crisps. When his mother came back from his room, carrying the empty laundry basket, he glared at her.

"I don't see why I have to do this," he growled. "It's ruining my afternoon."

"Well, perhaps your bad attitude is ruining my afternoon," his mother answered. "After you've finished there, I think you should go to your room and take a nap so you don't bring that sour behaviour to the dinner table."

"I'm not six. I don't need a nap."

"Then just lie there in your room and think about the way you're acting. Don't come out until you can put a smile on your face."

The Hoove was way ahead of Mrs Brownstone. While Rod was walking to the kitchen to hang up the hand vac, the Hoove hurried into Rod's room to check out what kind of misery he could cause him in there. He saw some real possibilities. He could empty his underwear drawer into the wastebasket. He could short-sheet his bed. And he could even sprinkle water on the bottom sheet, so when Rod laid down on it, it would be soaking wet.

When Rod came in, the Hoove was floating on the ceiling, watching to see what the big jerk would do first.

Rod closed the blinds and looked around to make sure no one was watching. Then he put a chair in front of his door and crept over to his bookshelf. He moved three volumes of the *Guinness Book of Sports Records*, reached behind them, and took out a wooden box.

It had a word chiselled on the front, and when the Hoove read that word, he knew he had Rod Brownstone right where he wanted him.

Chapter 11

The word chiselled on the box was BLANKIE.

Rod had carved it with his Boy Scout knife when he was ten years old to earn a badge in woodworking. He was too embarrassed to show it to anyone except the assistant scout leader who gave out the badges. Rod had made the box as a special hiding place for his favourite possession – a dollar-size swatch of blue satin, the last remaining piece of the baby blanket he had carried around with him every minute of the day. Once, when he was almost four years old, he had forgotten Blankie at home on a family ski weekend in the mountains north of Los Angeles. He cried so hard and for so long that they finally had to turn the car around and drive over a hundred miles back home so he could be reunited with his blanket.

Over the years, Blankie had suffered a lot of rips and tears from being dragged around. The only thing left was the corner piece of satin trim and a few centimetres of soft, furry blanket. But no matter how ragged it had become, Rod was attached like glue to his blankie. He took it out every night when he went to bed, holding it in his right hand and rubbing it back and forth on the tip of his nose. He couldn't fall asleep without it. And on occasions when he felt especially upset or nervous, like before a big football game, he'd take Blankie out for an emergency nose rub.

Rod had never told anyone about the existence of his blankie. It was his deep, dark secret. He would die if any of his football buddies knew that he couldn't go to sleep without it.

Hoover, a student of human nature, immediately understood how important it was for Rod to keep his secret deep and dark. He watched with glee as Rod took the tattered blanket piece out of its wooden box. He howled with laughter when Rod flopped on the bed, folded his pillow in half, and put the piece of blue satin against his nose and whispered, "OK, Blankie. Do your stuff."

The Hoove circled the room, doing an invisible victory dance in the air. His mind raced with all the possibilities of what that little piece of fabric could do. If used correctly, it would give Billy a perfect opportunity to put the Brownstone goon in his place.

Ah, Hoover thought. *Revenge is sweet.*

The Hoove waited impatiently for Rod to nod off into the nap he hadn't wanted to take and didn't feel he needed. Just to pass the time, Hoover amused himself by turning a few of the football pennants on the wall upside down and tying the laces of all of Rod's shoes together into a ball. After a few minutes, Amber stomped in.

"Mum wants you to set the table for dinner," she said, waking Rod up.

"You do it," he said with a yawn. "You need the practice."

"It's your turn, dingbat," she said. "And by the way, what is that in your hand?"

"Nothing," Rod answered, immediately shoving the blankie into the two halves of his folded pillow.

"It's not nothing. It's something. Otherwise you wouldn't have shoved it under your pillow. It looked like one of my doll blankets."

"Don't be an idiot," Rod snapped. "What would I want with a stupid doll blanket? Now get out. The sign on the door says 'private'."

"I know what it says," Amber answered, putting her pudgy hands on her hips. "I can read. In fact, I can even read your pennant upside down. It says 'Chargers Go!'"

"What are you talking about?" Rod said. "It's not upside down."

"Take a look, Mr Know-It-All."

Rod glanced at the wall. His "Go Chargers" pennant was indeed upside down.

"You did that just to annoy me, didn't you?" he snarled at Amber.

"I wouldn't come into your room for a million dollars," Amber said. "I have better things to do than watch you poke around in other people's lives with your spy cam."

"How many times do I have to tell you? I gather intelligence."

"No, you don't. You just spy."

The Hoove was thoroughly enjoying the conversation. Little Amber was a firecracker, and he was developing a real liking for her.

Feeling satisfied that she had won the argument, Amber left. As soon as she was gone, Rod snatched his blankie from under the pillow and stuffed it back in the wooden box. Holding the box behind his back, he crept over to the bookshelf and put it in its secret hiding place behind the Guinness records books. The Hoove could hardly wait to get his hands on it. It was all he could do to keep himself from pouncing on that blankie box. As soon as Rod left the room, he swooped over to the bookshelf and grabbed it.

"Oh yeah," he said to the box. "You and me, we're going to make some beautiful music together."

He tucked the box securely under his arm and shot through the wall, making it to the other side. However, in his excitement, he had completely forgotten that although he could travel through walls, earthly things made of matter could not. He found himself outside of the Brownstones' house, empty-handed. Looking through the window, he saw the wooden box lying on the rug where it had fallen when he passed through the wall.

Diving headlong back through the wall, the Hoove went back into Rod's room, glancing around to make sure he hadn't returned. The only activity he saw was Rod's Siamese fighting fish swimming around his bowl in alarmed circles.

"Hey, don't worry about it, big fin," the Hoove

said to him. "I'm not after you. Ghosts like fishies."

The Hoove picked up the blankie box from the carpet and zoomed over to the window. Throwing it open, he escaped into the evening air with his prized possession in his hand.

Chapter 12

Billy was in his room, working out with dumb-bells, when the Hoove burst in through the wall.

"Put those things down right away," he ordered Billy. "I have big news. A Bingo-Rama for the good guys."

"I can't put them down," Billy said, continuing to curl one weight at a time. "If I do, I won't be able to lift them up again. Besides, I have a rhythm going."

"Trust me. This is worth it."

"And trust me. My biceps are screaming for help. I can't ignore them now."

The Hoove hovered ten centimetres off the ground, getting right up in Billy's face.

"What am I holding behind my back?" he asked Billy. "Guess."

"I don't have to guess," Billy answered, the veins in his neck sticking out from his last set of curls. "I can see right through you. It's a box. What's so great about that?"

"Feast your eyes, Billy Boy, on a little bit of magnificence." With a flourish, the Hoove brought the box out from behind him. He opened it very slowly as if it contained the most valuable object in the world.

"OK, OK. Cut the drama. I'll look," Billy said. As he leaned down to place the dumbbells on the floor, their weight pulled him off his feet and he almost stumbled right into the box.

"Will you try to remain standing?" the Hoove said. "This is serious business."

"I didn't mean to fall. I'm just a little weak, which is why I'm lifting these stupid weights in the first place."

"Where you have been weak in the past, you will now be strong," the Hoove declared. "For in this box is the answer to all your problems. A magic carpet ride, so to speak. What do you see?"

Billy glanced into the open box.

"I see a little piece of an old blanket. Big deal."

"Right here we have an example of the main difference between you and me," the Hoove proclaimed, pointing one of his pale fingers at Billy.

"Other than the fact that I'm alive and you're dead? I'd say that's the main difference. Oh yeah, and breathing. That's another difference."

"Billy Boy, you are focused on the wrong things, as usual." The Hoove lifted Rod's blankie out of the box and waved it in front of Billy. "The difference," he went on, "is that you see a blanket before you. And me, I see possibilities."

"To do what? Go into the ratty old blanket business?"

"What if I told you that this piece of cloth

142

used to be Rod Brownstone's baby blanket and that he still takes it to bed with him every night?"

Billy laughed at the very idea. "I'd say that could never happen. He's too tough to need a blankie. That's more my style."

Billy bent down to pick up his dumbbells again, but the Hoove reached out to stop him.

"Just this afternoon, I happened to witness Rod rub this exact piece of cloth against his nose as he curled up in his beddy-bed," the Hoove explained.

"Seriously?"

"Seriously. And it gets even better. No one, not even his little sister, knows it exists."

Billy considered what the Hoove was telling him. Little by little, it began to dawn on him why the Hoove had presented his discovery of the blanket with so much drama. He was thinking of revenge, of getting even. And this piece of blanket held the key.

Billy's mind didn't naturally go to thoughts of revenge – that wasn't his nature. But the Hoove was showing him another path, a way to stand up for himself, and as his mind embraced the idea, his eyes lit up.

"I think I'm getting it," he whispered. "What you're holding in your hands is Rod's deepest secret and worst nightmare."

The Hoove let out a howling laugh.

"Just imagine, Billy Boy, what some of those cute girlies at your school, such as Ruby Baker, would think if they saw Mr Football Hero's baby blankie run up to the top of the flagpole."

A smile spread across Billy's face. The Hoove went on.

"Or how about if your mum came on the loudspeaker and announced that Rod's baby blanket had been turned in to the Lost and Found, and he could come pick it up whenever it was convenient for him."

"How would she know it belonged to him?" Billy asked.

"How did Ruby know that tonsil was yours? There was a note attached."

Suddenly, Billy was loving this conversation. His mind shifted into gear, and all kinds of spectacular revenge possibilities burst into his head, like a fireworks display on the Fourth of July.

"We could put up flyers all over school, announcing that it's lost," he began.

"Go on." The Hoove nodded. He was grinning broadly. "You're getting it."

"Or put it in the display case where the football trophies are," Billy went on. "We could tape a note to one of the trophies with an arrow that says, *I am Rod Brownstone's baby blankie. He loves me more than football*."

The Hoove laughed even harder. He was feeling victorious that finally Billy was getting some of the Porterhouse Attitude. Maybe there was hope for this kid yet.

"I like the train of thought you're riding on," he said to Billy. "Put it on full throttle and blow the whistle."

"OK, how's this for the best idea yet?" Billy

said. "We could spread the word about Rod's baby blankie and then charge admission to see it. Anyone who wants to take a look has to cough up a dollar."

"Brilliant," the Hoove said, snapping his suspenders the way he did when he felt everything was going his way. "We humiliate Brownstone just like he did to you AND we put some extra cabbage in our pockets at the same time."

Billy suddenly stopped laughing and looked perplexed. "Wait, Hoove. Why would we want to put a vegetable in our pockets?"

"Cabbage ... you know ... as in moolah. Money. What's the matter, don't you speak English?"

"Sure I do. Just not hundred-year-old English."

"You make a good point, ducky. Sometimes I forget I'm a hundred and thirteen. So what's it going to be? Flagpole? Flyers? Cabbage?"

Billy didn't know. He and the Hoove had

come up with so many revenge plots so quickly that his head was spinning.

"I have to take a break, Hoove, and clear my mind," he said. "I'll be back in a sec. I need some Gatorade."

"Gatorade?" the Hoove repeated. "Is that made directly from the alligator? Because if it is, count me out. I don't drink juice they have to squeeze a reptile for."

"Boy, you really are a hundred and thirteen years old!" Billy laughed. "Gatorade is a sports drink. I drink it when I need a burst of energy. Like now, when I have a lot of things to mull over."

"What's there to mull over? You're going pull off this plan, aren't you?"

Billy didn't answer. He had never really done anything like this before. Usually when he had a conflict with someone, he would take the easy way out and let the other person win. This new way would take a lot of courage. The Hoove saw Billy waffling, and moved in very close to him.

"Listen, Billy," he said, suddenly very serious.

"You have to stand up to this guy or he's not going to stop making you miserable."

"I'm going to get Brownstone," Billy said, suddenly sounding not so sure of himself. "At least I think I am. I just have to figure out how. I'll be right back with a solid plan."

Billy headed down the hall towards the kitchen, his mind racing. The idea of getting even with Rod was very appealing. Yet there was something gnawing at him. He wasn't entirely comfortable with the idea of revenge. He had been taught that two wrongs don't make a right. In the back of his mind, he wondered if embarrassing Rod Brownstone would make his situation any better.

Maybe he should just tell the Hoove to forget it. Maybe in time, the Great Tonsil Incident would become a distant memory for him and for everyone else.

As he rounded the corner into the kitchen, Breeze was finishing a phone conversation. She didn't look at all happy to see him.

"Thanks a lot," she said, before he had even reached the refrigerator.

"You're welcome. For what?"

"For putting an end to my band before we even got off the ground."

"Me? What did I do to your band?"

"For starters, no one wants to come over here to rehearse. Two of the girls, Sofia and Rachel to be specific, said they don't want to be in a house where people collect body parts. Oh, and in case you hadn't heard, since this afternoon, you apparently have a new nickname at school . . . Mr Tonsil. Or Big T, for short."

Billy felt like he had been punched in the stomach. He knew word of his tonsil had spread, but he had no idea *everyone* had heard about it, even the seventh graders. And that nickname. He would never, ever live it down if he stayed at Moorepark Middle School for two hundred years.

"I had no idea," he said, his voice cracking.

"A funny thing happens when you bring a

tonsil to school," Breeze said, shaking her head at how dense her new brother could be. "Word spreads fast. You might want to think about that next time you get a bright idea like that."

Billy wanted to sink through the speckled linoleum floor and disappear. All the embarrassment of the day came flooding back over him. Suddenly, he felt a surge of anger rising up in him like a powerful ocean wave. Rod had done this to him. Rod had ruined his life.

He knew what he had to do.

Without a word to Breeze, and forgetting entirely about the Gatorade he had come to get, Billy stormed back to his room, flung open the door, and announced to the Hoove, "I'm in."

Chapter 13

Billy didn't sleep a wink that night. He was too nervous. Never before in his life had he done something as brave or as bold as what he was about to do to Rod Brownstone. He was always the nice guy, looking for ways to solve problems, not cause them. He was a peacemaker, not a troublemaker.

"That was the old Billy Broccoli," the Hoove had said to him after he returned from the kitchen and they huddled in his room, formulating the plan. "The new Billy Broccoli fights fire with fire. The new Billy Broccoli lives the Hoove's Rule Number Eighty-six: 'The only way to handle a bully is to out-bully him.'"

So Hoover and the new Billy Broccoli got to work. The Hoove made Billy take out a piece of paper and list all of their ideas. There were eleven in total. Then they ranked each one according to how much it would embarrass Rod and how likely it was that Billy could actually pull it off.

They both agreed that Number 1 on the Embarrassment List was announcing on the loudspeaker that Rod Brownstone's baby blanket was flying on the flagpole and anyone who wanted to see it was invited to come outside and salute. To the Hoove's dismay, however, this idea ranked Number 11 on Billy's Ability to Pull It Off list. There was no way Billy could sneak into his mother's office, where the loudspeaker microphone was kept. And Billy would never be able to get the blanket up the flagpole because the raising of the flag was done every morning by Mr Yuki, the school groundskeeper. He was a gruff man who did not tolerate any nonsense. If you were walking on the lawn instead of the path, he'd turn the sprinklers on you without batting an eye.

"We'll have to go with Plan Number Two," Billy explained to the Hoove. "I'll tape a sign on the trophy case outside the attendance office, telling everyone that Rod's little baby blankie is available for viewing in the lunch pavillion."

The Hoove shook his head.

"The lunch pavillion lacks flair," he said. "It's what ordinary thinkers come up with. But the flagpole, now that has *style*. You don't want to just get this guy, Billy Boy. You want to get him with *style*. How bad could Mr Yuki be?"

"I'll show you," Billy said. "Wait here."

He went to Breeze's room and knocked.

"I'm out here," she called. She was sitting at the dining room table with Bennett, looking bored while he sifted through a box of dusty old papers.

"Come out and join us, Bill," Bennett called. "I was putting some things away in the garage and found these original maps of the property.

Breeze is fascinated with them, aren't you, honey?"

"It was this or algebra homework," Breeze explained when Billy shot her a look.

"Can I borrow your yearbook for a second?" Billy asked her.

"Only if you put it right back and promise not to read any of the notes from my friends, because they are extremely private."

As Billy headed back to his room with Breeze's yearbook, he wondered if anyone would ever write anything extremely private in his yearbook. Anything other than *You've got a humongous tonsil, Big T*, that is.

He took the yearbook to the Hoove and flipped through it until he found the section of staff pictures. There was one of Mr Yuki holding his prize oscillating lawn sprinkler and scowling at the camera. Even the Hoove had to acknowledge that he did indeed look like a man who meant business, sprinkler-wise and flagpole-wise.

Reluctantly, the Hoove abandoned the flagpole idea and agreed to settle on the trophy case plan. He and Billy sat at the computer and composed a note that was to be taped on the glass when no one was looking. Billy was shocked to see that the Hoove had excellent computer skills. He helped Billy pick a unique type style, changed the colour of each letter, and put fancy scrolls down the margins to make the note look like the Declaration of Independence.

"They didn't even have computers in your day," Billy said. "How'd you learn to do all this?"

"I may be dead, but I am not ignorant," the Hoove answered as he waited for the note to come out of the printer. "I'm what you'd call a life-long learner. If I had a life, that is."

"You taught yourself? How? Where?"

"There's a cosy little spot down the street they call the public library. I like to frequent it in the after-midnight hours. It's just me and one other ghost, so there's no wait for the computers."

Billy was amazed. He'd imagined that Hoover had a wild night life, doing ghostly things like flying around in the shadow of the moon and howling like a banshee and scaring random people in graveyards. A smile crossed his lips.

"Hey, what's so funny?" the Hoove asked.

"You in the library. I don't think of you as the library type. I thought you'd be out cruising around on broomsticks and stuff like that."

"Broomsticks are very slow and clunky, which is why only witches ride on them. Personally, I wouldn't be caught dead on a broomstick. Oh, wait, I *am* dead. Make that, I wouldn't be caught *alive* on a broomstick."

The Hoove howled with laughter at his own little joke. He was in a jolly mood. To his surprise, he had developed a real affection for Billy Broccoli, and he couldn't wait to see the joy on his face when he got even with Rod Brownstone and restored his own reputation.

When the note was finished, Billy placed it in his rucksack along with the wooden box containing the swatch of Rod's baby blanket. Then he and the Hoove went over the plan one more time. There was nothing left to do except for Billy to get a good night's rest. The Hoove, making an exception to his "no mornings" rule, said he would be back at exactly seven to make sure Billy was up and dressed in style for his big day. He disappeared through the door of Billy's room, and as he floated down the hall, Billy heard Breeze yell, "There's a cold draught in here. Will somebody please close their window?"

If she only knew, Billy thought. *She'd really be yelling.*

Billy got in bed, but as the minutes ticked into hours, he just lay there with his eyes wide open, staring at the ponies jumping over rainbows on his wallpaper. Dawn was breaking by the time Billy fell asleep. In the blue-grey light of his room, as his eyelids grew heavy and finally closed, Billy fell into a dream that he was shaking all over and someone was calling his name. His eyes flew open. It wasn't a dream.

The Hoove was hovering over him, shaking him vigorously and calling his name.

"Billy! Billy! Wake up, Billy Boy! You're not going to believe it!"

Billy rubbed his eyes and glanced at the clock on his pink and lavender bed stand. It was barely six o'clock.

"I don't have to get up for another hour," he muttered, and tried to turn over to avoid the Hoove, who was slapping his shoulder with a dusty old piece of paper.

"You know what this is?" the Hoove was saying. "Your stepfather, Bennett, is a genius. I love that guy, even with all his molar talk. Look what he's uncovered."

Billy's curiosity was aroused. He turned over and glanced at the rolled-up yellowing scroll in the Hoove's hand. He thought he saw a little spider crawl out of it and scurry across his bedsheet.

"Look at this," the Hoove said, unravelling the scroll and smoothing the paper with his

158

hands, which revealed a map that looked like it was hand-drawn in brown ink. "It's a map of our ranchero."

"Right," said Billy, sitting up to get a better look. "That's the old map Bennett found in the garage. So what?"

"See, here's the orange grove," the Hoove said, pointing to the largest section of the map. "And here's the barn. There's the corral, the original house, the toolsheds ... all four of them ... and the horse-shoeing shed. And way over there is the avocado orchard. I never knew the avocado orchard was part of our property. Can you believe it, Billy? This is, as you modern kids say, way cool. The avocado orchard!"

"What's the big deal?" Billy asked. "Do you have, like, a huge craving for guacamole or something?"

"I did used to love it with Lupe's home-made crisps," Hoover said. "But that's not the point. The point is that the avocado orchard is on our property. Which means I can travel there safely without dematerializing. And do you know what the avocado orchard has become, Billy? Do you?"

Billy studied the map carefully. The avocado orchard had a small road running through it. And although it was hard to read, if he looked carefully, he could see the fine print that said the road was called Moorepark Avenue.

"My school?" he asked.

"The very same," the Hoove said with a grin as big as a crate of oranges. "Moorepark Middle School. Slam-bam in the middle of the old avocado orchard. Which means, my friend, that I can go with you to school today. That the flagpole plan can be reinstated. We don't need your Mr Yuki to run Rod's blankie up the flagpole. I can do it for you."

And just to demonstrate, the Hoove drifted over to Billy's rucksack, took the piece of blanket out of its box, and floated up to the ceiling, waving the tattered old thing around like it was a pair of underpants fluttering on the clothesline.

The Hoove couldn't wait to put the plan in motion. He rustled Billy out of bed and practically threw him into the shower. While Billy was in the bathroom, Hoover changed the note so that it told kids to go outside and find the blanket waving on the flagpole. The Hoove was so jittery, he made Billy try on three different T-shirts until he found the one that was just right – a vintage shirt from the Brooklyn Dodgers, back when the team still played in New York. It wasn't really that old, but it was made of soft blue cotton and had some fake fraying around the collar that made it look authentic.

"Now you look dapper," he said to Billy, standing back to admire the outfit he had carefully selected. "So let's go to school and watch you go from a zero to a hero."

The Hoove followed Billy into the kitchen. He was itching to get on the road, and very annoyed that Billy had to stop for breakfast. But Billy had told him that there was no negotiating with his mother about breakfast, and if he tried to skip it, it would only provoke a lecture from her on how it's the most important meal of the day.

Billy's mother was surprised to see him at the breakfast table so early. She had heard about his tonsil, of course – nothing that happened at Moorepark Middle School escaped the head teacher's notice. But she had chosen not to say anything to Billy. He was already embarrassed enough without having to discuss the situation with his mother. Instead, she chose to give Billy a reassuring smile as she put a bowl of oatmeal and a glass of orange juice on the table for him.

"I'm happy to see you up and eager to go back to school, honey," she said, looking for her car keys, which she had left somewhere on the kitchen counter. "If you face trouble with a smile, everyone will respect you for it."

Billy tried not to consider what his mother would think if she knew what he was planning. He just nodded and took a spoonful of his oatmeal. The Hoove sat down on the chair next to Billy.

"Hurry up," he said. "You don't have to scrape the bowl."

Mrs Broccoli-Fielding found her car keys and came over to say goodbye to Billy. As she bent down to give Billy a kiss on the cheek, she got a strong whiff of the Hoove's orange grove aroma.

"Be sure to change your shirt before you leave," she said to Billy. "Somebody smells like he spilled orange juice on himself."

"See you later, Mum," Billy said.

"Be a good boy," she answered, then added, "What a silly thing to say. You always are."

"And that is exactly his problem," the Hoove said, although Mrs Broccoli-Fielding could not hear him, and certainly would not have agreed with him if she had.

By the time Billy had put his glass and bowl in the dishwasher, the Hoove was waiting for him at the back door, holding his rucksack. Hoover floated next to Billy as they walked to school. When they reached the corner of Moorepark Avenue and Avocado Lane, the Hoove stopped in his tracks.

"Hold it, ducky. I want to savour this moment."

Then he took a giant exaggerated step out into the street, over an imaginary line. He burst into a big smile.

"Victory!" he shouted. "This is the first time in ninety-nine years I've crossed over this line. Now I know how those astronauts felt, exploring new territory. One small step for the Hoove, one giant step for ghostkind."

Billy had to laugh. If he had to have his own personal ghost, Hoover Porterhouse was not a bad choice. He certainly was a lot of fun.

"Do you mind if I fly on ahead?" the Hoove asked Billy when they were still a block away from school. "I want to get there before you and check out the grounds. See where everything is. Get my game face on."

"Go right ahead," Billy said.

"So cough up the blankie," the Hoove said, holding out his hand. "I'm going to take it on a practice run up the flagpole, just to make sure there are no last-minute glitches."

Billy unzipped his rucksack and pulled the swatch of blue blanket out of its box. The Hoove wadded it up tightly so that it was no bigger than a marble. As he flew off, he whistled "I've Been Working on the Railroad", and it actually worked this time, making him invisible even to Billy. All he could see of the Hoove was the little blue ball of blanket travelling through the air, looking like a dandelion floating in the breeze.

Billy was actually relieved to be free of the Hoove for a while. He had to focus on what he was about to do. The old doubts were creeping in again, and he had to overcome them. This was no time to be soft on Rod Brownstone. Billy knew his reputation was at stake. Was he forever going to be the good little boy or was he finally going to stand up for himself?

He forced himself to concentrate on what the Hoove had taught him . . . that the only way to fight a bully was to out-bully him. He repeated that sentence over and over and over again as he turned the corner and walked up the steps and through the doors of Moorepark Middle School.

Chapter 14

The trophy case was located in the main hall between the head teacher's office and the attendance office. Every kid in school had to pass by it on the way to class. Billy approached the case cautiously, looking both ways down the hall. His stomach was doing somersaults as his mind began to grasp the risk he was about to take. It was not going to be easy to put the note up without being seen. He was going to have to look casual, like he was really interested in examining the school's athletic history, and at the same time, tape the note to the glass as quickly as he could.

Billy reached into the pocket of his sweatshirt. He pulled out the roll of Scotch tape he had hidden there, and did exactly what he had practised the night before, pulling off four equal strips that he attached to the tips of four of his fingers. Looking intently at the case, as though he had never seen a trophy before, he reached into his other pocket and pulled out the flyer, neatly folded into fourths. He looked around and noticed Ricardo Perez walking up to him.

Oh no, he thought to himself. *He's on to me. How could he possibly know what I'm doing?*

"Hey, man," Ricardo said to Billy. "You coming to baseball practice today?"

"Absolutely," Billy answered, stuffing his hand with the Scotch tape strips into his pocket. He was glad that Ricardo hadn't put out his hand for a high five. That would have been a very sticky situation.

"Got your gear?" Ricardo asked.

"Oh yeah. I have a whole plastic baggy full of pencils, a sharpener and a new score pad."

Ricardo squinted at Billy. "I thought you

wanted to make the team," he said. "Leave the pencils in your rucksack, dude. Show the coach you're a player."

Ordinarily, Billy would have welcomed this advice, but at the moment, all he wanted was for Ricardo to leave so he could get on with his mission.

"Thanks for the tip," Billy said. "I'll see you later. No pencils. That's a deal."

Ricardo nodded and walked off, joining some other members of the team as they headed for registration. Billy had to act fast, before anyone else noticed he was hanging around the display case. He unfolded the flyer and pulled his hand with the tape strips from his pocket. Unfortunately, all the strips stayed behind, having adhered to the inside fabric. Billy had no choice but to pull the roll of Scotch tape out and start all over again. His hands were shaking as he tore off four more strips.

"Move fast," he said to himself. "Like a Scotch tape ninja."

That didn't make much sense, but the image did the trick for Billy. He deftly tore off the four strips and was just about to put the flyer in place against the glass, when he felt someone tapping on his shoulder. Billy spun around to see none other than Rod Brownstone standing next to him.

"Hey, Broccoli, back off the glass. You're leaving breath marks. Some of those trophies are mine, and I don't want you contaminating the display."

Billy looked at Rod and realized that he looked a mess. His usually combed black hair was tangled. He had dark circles under his eyes, and his clothes looked slept in.

"You're not looking too good this morning," Billy said to him. "Have a rough night?"

"I couldn't sleep. What's it to you?"

Billy shot him a mysterious little smile.

"Word on the street is that you lost something," he said.

"How do you know?" Rod answered. "Tell me the truth, Broccoli, or I'll lock you in this case and throw away the key."

"Really, Rod? Are you all that tough? Because I never heard of a tough guy needing his" – and now Billy lowered his voice to a whisper – "baby blankie."

"How do you know about that? Have you been spying on me?"

"If I did, I learned from the master. You're not the only one with intelligence."

All the colour drained out of Rod's face. Suddenly, he didn't look so tough any more. In fact, he looked scared. With newfound courage, Billy took advantage of the moment.

"Tell me, Rod," he said with a grin. "Do you suck your thumb, too, or is rubbing Blankie on your nose all you need to put you to sleep?"

"You saw me?"

"Personally, no. But my source tells me you don't look like much of a football player when you're all curled up with Mr Blankie."

"You're not going to tell anyone about this, are you, Broccoli?"

"No, I'm not going to tell anyone. I'm just

going to invite everyone to view it. To see a piece of the great Rod Brownstone's cute little blue satin baby blanket."

"You have it? So you're the one who stole it?"

"No, actually, I've never even been in your room. But I have my own unique way of acquiring evidence."

"You're a thief," Rod said.

"No, that would be you – who took the tonsil jar right out of my room and brought it to school to humiliate me. So now I'm going to return the favour and humiliate you right back."

"I wouldn't do that if I were you," Rod said, moving his hulking body right up next to Billy, getting in his face in a threatening way. "Hand it over, toadface, or I'll flatten you into a pancake."

But for the first time in his life, Billy wasn't backing down. He thought of what the Hoove had taught him – that he had to face this guy once and for all. Now all he wanted was to stand his ground and make Rod feel the embarrassment and shame he had felt.

"You're too late, Rod, because it's almost done. The plan is in motion. See this note? It tells the entire student body to go outside and see your little blankie, which in a few minutes is going to be hoisted to the top of the flagpole."

"This will ruin me," Rod groaned.

"Oh, really? Just like you ruined me when you took my tonsil and made me the laughing stock of the school?"

"That was different."

"How do you figure that? Because it happened to me? That's the trouble with creeps like you. You don't care that you made me feel bad, that everyone made fun of me. Well, now you're going to know what it feels like. And trust me, Brownstone, it doesn't feel good."

"Don't do this, Broccoli. I'll do anything if you just keep quiet and give me the blanket back."

This offer caught Billy quite by surprise. It had never occurred to him that he could turn this terrible situation into something positive. Suddenly, an entirely different plan popped into his mind.

"I might consider halting the plan under certain circumstances," he said to Rod. "If you meet my demands, I will take this flyer and give it to you. No one ever has to know about our little secret."

"Tell me what you want," Rod begged. Billy thought it looked like he was about to cry. He had Rod right where he wanted him.

"First, I want you to tell Ruby Baker that the whole thing was your idea. That you planted the tonsil in front of her. That you wrote the note."

"OK," Rod said. "She's in my first-period class. I'll go and tell her straight away."

He started to leave, but Billy grabbed him by the shoulder and pulled him back.

"I'm not finished yet," he said. "Second, and most important, I want a public, all-school apology."

"What do you want me to do?" Rod was whining now. "Go up to every student and individually tell them? I can't do that."

"We happen to have a very fine public address system in this school." Billy smiled. "And I have an in with the head teacher. I think I might be able to talk her into letting you use it."

"I can't," Rod said.

"Fine, that's your choice," Billy said. "And now if you'll excuse me, I have to go outside to the flagpole and fly something that's very close to you from the top of it."

Billy turned and started down the hall towards the front door. Before he had taken five full steps, he felt Rod's hand on his shoulder.

"You win," Rod said. "I'll do it. I won't like it, but I'll do it. Now give me Blankie back."

"I'll meet you back here in five minutes," Billy said. "I have to find my source to get it back. He prefers his identity to remain secret."

"I'm coming with you."

"Didn't you hear what I said, Brownstone? I told you to stay here, and I'm not kidding. That's part of the deal."

Rod started to pace back and forth, biting his nails and spitting out the clippings. Billy left him there and ran down the hall towards the front door. He felt like Superman without the cape. He had done it. He had surprised himself and stood up for what he knew was right. And he did it without becoming just like Rod. That felt powerful indeed.

Billy heard the bell ring as he ran down the front steps, two at a time. That meant he'd be late to registration, but in this case, it was a good thing. Everyone else would be in class, and he could talk to the Hoove without being seen. He looked around and saw no one.

"Hoove!" he called out. "Make yourself visible."

Billy heard a whistling from around the top of the flagpole. It was the familiar tune that he was beginning to get accustomed to – "I've

Been Working on the Railroad". Billy looked up and saw the Hoove start to appear in stages . . . first his belly, which looked pretty weird floating up there by itself. Then his right leg, followed by his neck and the other leg.

"Stop messing around and concentrate," Billy called to him. "I need to talk to you . . . *all* of you."

"Trust me, this is the best I can do," the Hoove said. Then he whistled a little more, and suddenly, the rest of his body and his face appeared. He was sitting on the brass ball on top of the flagpole.

"Get down here," Billy called to him. "And bring the blanket with you. There's been a change of plans."

The Hoove slid down the pole, letting out a playful whoop as he did. When he reached the ground, he floated over to Billy and snapped his suspenders.

"I should have been a fireman," he said. "Turns out I'm good at pole sliding."

"Hand over the blanket," Billy said, talking very quickly. "We're giving it back. Rod is waiting for me at the trophy case, practically biting his finger off."

The Hoove looked extremely distressed. "You caved in to that bully. What'd he do, threaten you? I'm going in there to take care of him once and for all."

The Hoove took off, gliding through the air towards the school entrance.

"I didn't cave," Billy called after him. "I got exactly what I wanted. He's going to tell Ruby I didn't give her the tonsil, and apologize to the whole school over the loudspeaker."

The Hoove came to a sudden stop, as though he had slammed on an invisible brake.

"Wait a minute," he said, flying back to where Billy was standing. "That's good. Very good. How'd you do that?"

"With your help. I could never have convinced him without you flying through walls to get the blanket for me. You got the plan started."

"That I did."

"And I finished it. With style, I might add. Just like you taught me."

"Like I always say, the Hoove's rules rule."

"You showed me how to believe in myself, Hoove. And that made me able to stand up to Rod. Before I met you, I didn't even think this was possible. And now look. I got the guy begging for his Blankie back."

Hoover tucked the little piece of blanket into his pocket.

"Well, he's not getting it back. We were on the way to bringing the big boy down, Billy. Can't we just let it flap in the breeze for a little while?"

"I gave him my word. Now give it to me, Hoove."

"I want you to know that my entire body, or lack of body, is vibrating against this decision."

"I know, Hoove. But trust me, for a change. It's the right thing to do."

"That does not come easy to me."

179

Billy looked the Hoove right in the eye until the Hoove couldn't stand it any more. Slowly, he reached into his trouser pocket and pulled out the little blue wad of blanket.

"We could have had such fun together," he said to the blanket. Then he handed it over to Billy.

No sooner was the blanket in Billy's hand than there was a roar of an aeroplane overhead. Billy and Hoover looked up. There was no aeroplane to be seen, but written in the sky, in a trail of white smoke, were the words:

HELPING OTHERS: SHOWS IMPROVEMENT.

And as suddenly as those words appeared, they were gone.

"Look at that," the Hoove said. "There's hope for me. That's the best report card I've ever had."

"Stick with me," Billy said.

"What choice do I have?" the Hoove answered. "You're my assignment."

As Billy stuffed the blanket into his pocket

and hurried up the stairs to school, the Hoove hovered in mid-air, watching him go. He noticed a look of confidence about Billy, an attitude he hadn't seen before.

"Maybe there's hope for that kid after all," he said.

But Billy, being Billy, ran smack into the door frame, bumping his forehead and spilling the contents of his rucksack all over the bricks. He looked up at the Hoove and waved, as if to say, "I'm all right."

"No waving," the Hoove called out to Billy. "Nowhere in the rules does it say it's OK to wave."

But Billy wasn't listening. He just continued to wave until the Hoove had no choice but to flick him a little wave back.

As Billy disappeared inside the school doors, Hoover Porterhouse shook his head and sighed. It was going to be one tough year.

Can't get enough of Billy and the Hoove?
Read on for a sneak peek at their
next crazy adventure!

Mind if I Read Your Mind?

"Who wants to go first?" Mr Wallwetter said, his beady eyes scanning the classroom like an eagle searching for a big, fat snake to eat. "Do we have a volunteer?"

"I nominate Cheese Sauce here," Rod Brownstone blurted out, pointing to Billy with his beefy index finger. Some of the kids in the class sniggered, but Billy ignored them. Growing up with the last name of Broccoli, he had got very good at ignoring cheese sauce jokes.

"How about it, Billy?" Mr Wallwetter said. "Why don't you be our first speaker in the Speak

Out Challenge. SOC it to 'em, if you catch my drift?"

Billy gulped. The Hoove still hadn't shown up, and without him, Billy had no speech. The assignment was to give a demonstration, and the Hoove was the main ingredient in his demonstration. He was going to have to stall until the Hoove arrived . . . that is, if he ever *did* arrive.

"Thanks so much for the offer, Mr Wallwetter," Billy said, using his most charming voice and sociable smile, "but I'd rather go last, if that works for you."

"It doesn't," Mr Wallwetter answered tartly, tugging on his skinny little moustache.

"Then how about next to last? I can make that work."

"Come right up to the front of the class now, Billy," Mr Wallwetter said in a way that didn't leave much room for saying no. "Wow us all with your demonstration."

Billy looked around desperately for signs of the Hoove, hoping that he had floated in and was hovering somewhere above the fluorescent lights. No such luck. Billy's heart raced with a combination of anger and nerves. The Hoove had sworn he'd be there when the opening bell rang. Promised. On his honour.

"The Hoove's Rule Number One Hundred Forty-three," he had declared just that morning. "When you count on the Hoove, you can count on the Hoove."

Yeah, right, Billy thought. *I'd do better counting on my fingers and toes.*

As Billy shuffled reluctantly to the front of the class, Rod made farting sounds with his mouth in time to Billy's steps. Mr Wallwetter didn't seem to notice, though. He was busy writing Billy's name on the board, along with the topic he had submitted.

A Demonstration of Mind Reading by William C. Broccoli.

"Check it out," Brownstone snorted. "I bet that *C* stands for Cheese Sauce."

"Honestly, Rod, why don't you knock it off already," Ruby whispered to him. "It wasn't even funny the first time."

Billy smiled at Ruby and she smiled back. *Enjoy it while you can*, he thought. In about two minutes, that great smile of hers was going to vanish when he made a total dork of himself trying to demonstrate mind reading and coming up with zippo.

"Are you ready, Billy?" Mr Wallwetter asked, putting down the chalk and walking over to his desk.

"We were born ready, weren't we, Billy Boy?" came a ghostly voice from the back of the room. Billy looked up and there, swooshing through the door in his hyperglide mode, was Hoover Porterhouse.

"I was about to give up on you, pal," Billy said aloud before he could stop himself.

Mr Wallwetter, not knowing there was a ghost in the room, thought Billy was addressing him. "Well, I'll never give up on you, pal," he whispered, coming over to Billy and giving his shoulder a reassuring squeeze. "Show us what you got, buddy."

"Let's do this," the Hoove said. "We're going to make their heads spin!"

Henry Winkler & Lin Oliver

Ghost Buddy

Mind if I Read Your Mind?